MAID FOR THE BEAST

INTERSTELLAR BRIDES® PROGRAM: THE BEASTS - 2

GRACE GOODWIN

GET A FREE BOOK!

JOIN MY MAILING LIST TO BE THE FIRST TO KNOW OF NEW RELEASES, FREE BOOKS, SPECIAL PRICES AND OTHER AUTHOR GIVEAWAYS.

http://freescifiromance.com

FIND YOUR INTERSTELLAR MATCH!

YOUR mate is out there. Take the test today and discover your perfect match. Are you ready for a sexy alien mate (or two)?

1

Angela Kaur, 5 Star Hotel, Secret Location, Miami, Florida

I ROLLED the cart down the hall, steering it to the side and pausing as two women passed. Their heads were bent close, and the two whispered and laughed to each other.

"I'm going to be the one to let that beast out," I heard one say.

The other giggled, then replied, "You mean that beast in his pants."

They didn't even look my way. To them, I was invisible. When compared to them, I was. Their hair was done, makeup perfect. Cute outfits. Even cuter shoes.

I had on utilitarian black sneakers with more insole than fashion sense. They were as drab as the black skirt and white blouse of the uniform I wore. I pushed on down the hall and stopped at the Presidential Suite, the toilet bowl brush handle clacking against the side of the bucket it was in, hidden beneath the thick fabric on my housekeeping cart. Folded towels towered on the top, and I could barely see over it. Bad luck of being five feet nothing.

I'd been cleaning since early this morning, and the suite was the last—and biggest—room. Then I'd be done for the day. I needed to go home, feed Oscar—before he destroyed another pair of my shoes—and try to figure out how I was going to afford to take two classes next semester and pay rent on my newish apartment while working fewer hours.

Work less, spend more. That seemed to be my motto lately.

Sighing, I tugged the polyester collar away from my neck, then knocked on the door.

Waited.

I knocked again, then called, "Housekeeping!"

The elevator chimed, and I turned to see two more pretty women step out. This was the floor where all the staff and participants of the *Bachelor Beast* show were being pampered and coached on their appearances. Not that these women needed any help with looking fabulous. I did not envy them. The competition was fierce, and I had no interest in trying to make some idiot man fall in love with me. Been there. Done that. And what a damn disaster.

This would be even worse. Twenty-four stunning contestants vying for one hulking alien from Atlan... and the beast in his pants. And doing it in front of a live television audience? No freaking way, thank you. I didn't care how smoking hot the alien bachelor might be.

Speaking of sexy bachelors, the door I knocked on once more belonged to the hulking alien from Atlan, here to find his bride.

He, along with the ladies, been here for a few days, but

today was my first shift cleaning on the executive level since their arrival.

I gave one last knock, called out, then pulled the universal key card from my pocket and slipped it into the lock. The little light turned green, and I pushed the door open.

"Housekeeping," I called one last time. I'd been in the suite to clean before—I'd worked at the hotel for three years —but had forgotten how large it was. There were two bedrooms off each side of a large living area that had a dining table and a small kitchen. Marble floors and even a fireplace made it nicer than any house I'd been in. Heck, my entire apartment could probably fit in one of the opulent bathrooms.

The main room was neat, as if no one had even moved the TV remote on the coffee table. I sighed, pleased to know it wouldn't be a miserable cleaning job. With both bedroom doors closed, I couldn't be too sure. The bathrooms were usually the biggest mess, and this suite had two.

With one of the suite's rooms just needing vacuuming, I could clock out on time today and get off my feet. Take a shower so I didn't smell like cleaning products.

I went out to the cart, grabbed the usual stack of fresh towels and mini-soaps, then returned, the door clicking shut behind me. I shivered. The air conditioner must be set to the lowest setting. I had to assume the Atlan didn't like Florida heat.

Picking the bedroom on the right to tackle first, I opened the door and stopped in my tracks.

My mouth dropped to the floor and so did the little soaps as they slipped off the top of the towels I held. I'd interrupted guests before and offered a quiet murmur of apology and backed out. Businessmen sprawled in their underwear, watching TV and eating from the minibar. Couples going at it who never even broke stride at my disturbance. But this guest?

Holy. Hell.

I'd seen the *Bachelor Beast* show. What woman would forget how the gorgeous Wulf had found his mate offstage, tossed her over his shoulder and carried her off to a dressing room. To have sex. Insane Atlan beast sex. It had been romantic and hot as hell.

Oh, the network couldn't show the actual *going at it* part, but Chet Bosworth had certainly filled in the blanks with suggestive commentary. Wulf had been huge. Hulking. Hot. Dominant. Wickedly possessive. Caring. All the adjectives that made every woman's ovaries pop out an egg or two.

But this guy? This Atlan?

Wow.

I'd seen the promos for the second season of the show and Braun, the next bachelor. Those Atlans had fantastic genetics, because the photos and video clips didn't do him justice. Not one little bit.

Heck, there wasn't anything *little* on him.

I knew that for fact because he'd just come out of the bathroom—ducking his head to fit through the doorway and turning his shoulders because they were just *that* broad —backlit by the vanity lights and surrounded by steam that had escaped the opulent room. In a towel. And just a towel.

An Earth-sized towel.

On an Atlan body.

I was very familiar with the large bath sheets. I folded and stacked them my entire shift. But while this one made it around his waist, the material barely tucked in and left his thigh exposed with a huge slit. And that thigh? It was probably as big as my waist.

It was like a human guy wrapping a dish towel about him.

Droplets of water slid down Braun's torso, and I watched their path. My mouth watered to lick them up.

Heat flared and I panicked, realizing I was frozen like a statue and ogling a guest.

A seven-foot-tall, gorgeous guest.

Who was staring right back. He raised one hand and pushed his wet hair back from his face as his dark gaze raked over me.

I swallowed, then dashed to the bed, set the towels on it, now trying to look anywhere but at him. "I'm so sorry. I didn't mean to disturb. A few towels." Stepping back, I stepped on one of the little soaps, the wrapper startling me, and I jumped.

He moved then. Fast. Too fast for someone his size, and grabbed my elbow.

"Careful."

His voice was deep and reverberated through me. His touch was gentle, the heat from his fingers seeping through my uniform. I had to tilt my head so far back to look up at him that I felt tiny.

Flustered now, I stepped back again, then bent down to grab the soaps I'd dropped.

A growl rumbled through him, making me pop right back up again.

His brow was furrowed, his eyes narrowed, his jaw clenched, and I'd just shoved my ass in his face.

I'd made him angry. What an idiot.

"I'm so sorry."

Great. I'd made the star of the *Bachelor Beast* upset. I was going to get fired for sexual harassment, and I couldn't let that happen. Sure, being a maid wasn't my dream job, but it paid the bills and would pay for my last two semesters of nursing school.

I turned to face him again, then backed up as if retreating after curtseying to the queen. "I'm so sorry to disturb you, sir. I will step outside. Please notify the front desk when you are ready to have your room cleaned."

I backed up again.

He stepped toward me.

I backed up once more in the direction of the suite's entry door.

"Who are you?" he asked.

I couldn't look him in the eye.

"I'm the maid."

"A maid," he said as if the word *maid* wasn't in his language. I was mortified at how I'd stared at him. Mostly naked. But *not* looking him in the eye meant I took in his muscular chest, the abs of epic steel. He had a dusting of golden hair between the flat disks of his nipples that tapered into a triangle to his navel, then to a thin line that disappeared beneath the towel and I could only imagine surrounded his—

Big cock.

My eyes widened as I saw the thick outline of it pressing against the towel... and lifting it.

Another growl ripped from him, and it startled me out of my stupor. Again.

"You clean for guests of the *Bachelor Beast* program?"

I gave an efficient nod. "And other rooms."

"I do not need you to do such tasks for me."

I nodded again, feeling more like a bobble doll by the minute. "Okay. Fresh towels are on your bed. Call down to the front desk if you need anything else."

I had my hand on the knob.

"Where are you going?"

I frowned, looked up—way up—into his light eyes. "You said you didn't need me to clean your room."

"That is correct. What is your name?" I watched as his gaze raked over my body. I thought of the two ladies I'd walked past earlier, the women who had talked about Braun so crudely. He'd be attracted to either one of them. I wasn't ashamed of my work, but there were moments when I didn't want to be invisible, didn't want to clean up other people's messes. Didn't want to be in the polyester uniform that was not styled for my round, petite physique. There wasn't a pastry I didn't like, and no matter how much exercise I tried—which wasn't much since my legs were short and my boobs needed two sports bras—I wasn't losing weight.

He studied my shoes, my legs below the black skirt, the black button-down top. My name tag, which made me remember his question.

I tapped the plastic pin above my left breast. "I apologize again."

I fled then, realizing I was in big, big trouble. I tossed the soaps I'd just remembered I was holding onto the dining table and took off.

Abandoning my housekeeping cart, I bolted for the service elevator at the far end of the hall. Fortunately there was no one around.

"Wait!" the deep voice boomed.

He was following me. Oh God, this was bad. He was the

most VIP of VIPs staying at the hotel. How could I have angered someone so special he wasn't even from Earth?

I'd get down to the housekeeping area in the basement and beg one of my coworkers to claim my cart.

I pushed the call button.

"Wait!" Braun said again, this time much closer. "Why are you running away?"

I spun about, tears in my eyes. I couldn't fight them. He was gorgeous. I was nothing. I'd made him angry. God, I'd never had a guest chase me down before.

"I caught you coming out of the shower. I'm sorry for invading your privacy."

"How do you invade privacy? My English is not strong, but that is confusing."

I frowned.

"Mr. Braun, I will have the head of housekeeping come to your room and ensure you are well satisfied with the hotel's service."

He looked me over again. "I am well satisfied with my maid, I assure you. If you remain, you can be satisfied as well."

I blushed, my mind going right to the gutter.

Did he mean what I thought? Satisfied? I closed my eyes and fought to hold back the shiver that raced up and down my spine, made my nipples pebble like twin, diamond-hard peaks.

The elevator dinged, thank God.

I shook my head. "I must go."

"No."

No? I heard the doors open behind me, and I spun and dashed inside and pushed the button for the basement.

Turning, I faced the Atlan, and I watched his face as he realized the door was going to close.

Behind him, a handful of ladies had heard the commotion and were coming out into the hallway. Their reaction to the view was causing a stir. As I watched, three more women appeared, every one of them heading in Braun's direction.

"I'm so sorry." The elevator door began to slide closed, and I saw one perfectly manicured, smooth-skinned hand wrap around Braun's biceps from behind. Bloodred nails, bright blue eyes, and midnight black hair. She was room 1214. I knew specifically because she had called the head of housekeeping insisting on three extra little shampoo and conditioner bottles every day. She looked like a real-life princess.

Hell, maybe she was.

"Braun? Everything all right?" 1214 asked, her voice making me cringe. So cultured and perfect. Like she'd grown up going to boarding school with the queen of England.

"No." He shrugged off her touch and dashed for the doors, to stop the elevator or climb on, I had no idea. In his rush, the towel slipped from his waist. As the doors slid closed, I got to see every inch of the Atlan beast.

Including the one between his legs.

arlord Braun, Twelfth Floor Hallway

I'D FOUND HER. My mate. The beautiful, dark female who'd appeared in my room.

I'd learned from Warlord Wulf that the moment he became aware of Olivia, his beast had chosen and there had been no doubt, no regret, only peace with his choice.

Olivia, his human mate, had laughed and said it was something called magic, a mystical notion that humans believed in. I hadn't understood either one of them, but now it made sense.

My mate had appeared as if by magic, as if I'd... conjured her from the last shards of hope holding me together.

No, not hope. Discipline. Restraint. I'd kept the beast at bay for years now, the Atlan curse of mating fever a constant fire in my blood. Yet I maintained my ice-cold control at all times. To allow a single act of rebellion by my beast would be to surrender completely.

And that I could not do, for the beast would not submit to me once he was free. He would rend and tear and destroy anything and everything in his way—except her.

Palms flat on the cold elevator doors, I took several deep breaths and fought him back into the pit of hell inside me where I'd kept him chained for too long. Month after painful month he had calmed when I held Caroline's and Rezzer's twins. He calmed when any of the children laughed and played nearby. My beast would never rage when an innocent child was about. But even that had begun to lose effect.

The last few months he simply raged within. The mental walls I'd built to keep him under control were thin. Dangerously so.

If I did not find a female to bind to him, he would force me to choose execution. The strength and fighting rage of an Atlan warlord was both gift and curse.

I needed my mate, the mating cuffs around my wrists. And hers. My beast required a female to serve and protect. To pleasure. To anchor both beast and male to this world. Well, not Earth, but *with* me. And he had chosen.

And yet she'd fled. The maid, our mate, had slipped through our fingers.

Unable to contain the explosion of emotion the beast threw at me, I opened my mouth and roared at the closed door. Just once. The beast wanted her to know, to hear, to answer his claim.

Fuck. I pressed my forehead to the cool metal and tried to calm the fuck down, my beast fighting tooth and nail to rip open the door with our bare hands, jump down the elevator shaft and *take her* somewhere safe. Somewhere she could learn us. Somewhere quiet and secluded and perfect for making her ours.

Ever since I'd been on Earth surrounded by females I'd immediately known were not mine, the beast's vexation had grown exponentially worse. I was irritable, frustrated. Annoyed. These twenty-four females who'd been chosen for the *Bachelor Beast* program were just as Wulf had described. Some arrogant and shallow. Some curious about alien males. Some kind. All truly beautiful.

My beast wanted none of them.

I was pleased to know that through the craziness of an Earth entertainment program, there were human females eager to find a match with a worthy Coalition fighter, even those from The Colony, but it was different when all of them chased *me*.

They were like Hive interceptors, circling and waiting to strike.

Even now as I stood staring at the closed elevator doors —my mate now gone somewhere else in the hotel—I knew they were lining the long hall. The entire floor was reserved for those participating in the television program.

Behind me the female—Priscilla was her name—lurked. Waiting. I recognized her cloying scent even without turning around.

My beast was highly attuned to our mate already. He had seen the frown on her face, the disapproval in her gaze when the bothersome contestant had touched me. We had upset our mate by allowing that touch, even if for only a moment.

A soft rustle of clothing and I knew Priscilla was moving, ready to try her luck again.

"Do not touch me, female," I warned. I refused to face her, hoping she'd just disappear.

She gasped but stepped back. "I'm sorry, I was just—"

Her words trailed off, but I did not care to hear them anyway. Her intentions were clear. Seduction. She didn't understand Atlans. She'd already lost the competition and it hadn't even started. My beast wanted nothing to do with her. My beast was interested in only one female now.

One.

Mine. Mine. Mine. The beast chanted inside my head and I could not get him to shut the fuck up.

I wanted to rip the metal elevator doors open, but I knew my mate would not be there. I had learned about the lift concept when I arrived. How primitive the machines were on Earth.

My cock was hard. My beast was pushing to the surface, eager to chase our mate down. Taste her. Touch her. Carry her back to the suite and fuck her. I'd hold her gently against the wall, her legs wrapped around my waist. She was so small I wondered if she'd even be able to cross her ankles at my lower back.

I gripped the base of my cock and gave it one firm stroke. Yes, she'd be eager. Soft. Lush. Wet. I wouldn't have to worry about crushing her with those full curves. I'd be cushioned as I took her. As I claimed her as mine.

She would accept my mating cuffs, and I would take her away from this primitive planet. Unlike any of the Earth females on The Colony, she had stunning dark skin, like the deepest of Prillon skin tones. Her hair was as black as the outer reaches of space, so thick and long that I could wrap it around my fist and hold her in place for my kiss.

Fuck! I pumped my cock once more, but it didn't ease

my need. Nothing would but claiming my mate. I'd been
waiting for her my entire life, and now I'd found her.

Three days. I'd been on this backward planet for three
days. I'd expected to begin the program immediately, but
Chet Bosworth, the annoying little human who was called
the host, had gotten some weird human ailment called pink
eye and refused to appear on camera until it was gone.

There were no ReGen wands here, so I was told it would
take days for Chet to be healed. I'd practically ripped my
hair out at the delay. I'd commed Wulf and grumbled. I'd
even complained to Governor Maxim and made my dissatis-
faction at being *volunteered* to be the next bachelor beast
thoroughly known.

He'd been trying to help me. I'd been bride tested but
had not been matched. Now I wanted to kiss the governor
because he'd been right. I'd found my mate here on Earth.
Because of the ridiculous show. Just like Wulf, she hadn't
been a contestant.

I didn't even know her name. I didn't know where she'd
gone. Running my hand through my hair, I spun around.
My beast was pushing me to find her. She was within the
building. I'd search every floor. I was panting, and my fists
clenched.

Then I saw the females who stood outside their rooms
all along the floor. The hideous multitoned carpet and gold
walls made me miss Base 5's plain design even more.

The females practically gasped in unison as I faced
them, my cock in hand. Their mouths were either hanging
open or in broad grins. Their gazes were fixed on my cock.
Every single one of them. Priscilla, who had dared touch
me, stepped back.

She was bold, but she was not stupid.

"Hey, big guy, do you need help with that?" another asked. Her blonde hair was long and sleek down her back. She was thin enough that I questioned her nutritional intake while the size of her breasts made me think any child she birthed would not go hungry.

I'd met her before. Ginger or Grace or Gabby. Something with a G.

It was her grating words that had me realizing I was naked. Cock in hand. In the hallway.

Fuck. Me.

I let my cock go, although it didn't drop since it was so fucking hard.

"What, exactly, is a maid?" I asked her.

Her eyes widened as I got closer. She was trying to look me in the eye, but her gaze kept dropping to my body. I wasn't the least bit modest. She could look her fill for all I cared. She wasn't touching me, nor would she. The beast would not have it.

"A maid?" she asked with a frown. "Someone who cleans."

"Why can't humans clean for themselves?" I asked.

She grinned, then winked at me. "You don't look dirty to me, but I'd be happy to assist if you need help getting clean."

Wulf's new mate, Olivia, rolled her eyes often. So did other human females on The Colony. I was tempted to make the same gesture now. "Why?" I asked through gritted teeth.

"Because you're gorgeous."

My beast wanted to growl at her and make her run from us. But that wouldn't help either of us, and we needed answers. "Why maids?"

"Why does the hotel have maids?" Two other contestants joined her, and they ogled me as a trio now.

I nodded. I had to find my mate, and if getting the information out of these females was required, I'd do it. No matter how painful it was.

"We're not at home. This is like a vacation. So someone else gets to do the dirty work," the blonde said.

The woman beside her—just as beautifully dark-skinned as my mate—nodded, then added, "Because that's their job."

I was not accustomed to someone being a servant to me. That's what my mate's employment was, even if the title on Earth was called *maid*. Servants on Atlan were respected and valued as part of the family. Everyone held positions of work and they were seen as equal, but based on the tone and the entitled dismissal of those who served them, these two females' answers had me disliking them immensely. It was one thing not to want to claim a female, another entirely not to respect them.

"Did the maid not leave you any towels or something? I've got some in my room," the dark female offered. "You can have anything you'd like in there."

The double meaning was not lost on me. She made a similar move to Priscilla, her hand drawing dangerously close to my arm.

I stepped away. No female would touch me but my mate.

"No, I have fresh towels in mine," the blonde countered, raising her hand to set it on my chest.

I flinched back. I would never harm a female, but these three were testing my patience. A well-placed roar, perhaps a solid growl would force them to learn a little respect.

Was this how they treated human males? Like a piece of

meat to fight over? As a prize to be won? A thing to conquer rather than a worthy male of honor? Not one of them had asked a single question of me. They knew nothing of my family, the war, or my past.

Perhaps they did not even know my name, for not one had deigned to use it.

If so, it was a wonder every male on the planet had not already volunteered to serve in the Coalition Fleet to escape them.

And yet... the human females I knew, those mated to other warriors, were not like these females. I would assume my mate would be more like Olivia and Caroline rather than the human animal called *vultures* circling me now.

"Do the maids return on some sort of schedule?" I had yet to see one before my mate's appearance. The past few days I'd been in interviews and other odd meetings for the program. I'd even had to be fitted for Earth clothing in my size.

They nodded in unison. "Every morning."

"Um... why are you standing in the hall naked?" the blonde asked.

I looked down at myself, wanted to roll my eyes. Again. I stepped around the females and went to my suite, the door swinging shut behind me. I let out a bellow that rattled the windows.

I had twenty-four females lingering in the hallway outside my room, and yet the one I wanted had fled. But she would return. Tomorrow.

The wait would be agony. I should storm through the hotel and find her. My beast loved that idea. But she'd fled when my beast hadn't been in charge. If I let him take over, I might scare her off forever.

No, I'd have her come to me. I'd be patient. Fuck, I wasn't sure how I'd do it, but I would. I'd do anything for my mate, including wait. I had already waited years. What were a few more hours?

My beast didn't like the way I was thinking. In fact, he raged. Paced. Fought to break free and destroy everything and everyone in our way. He *needed* her. Survival instinct was kicking in, and I had to lean over, hands on my knees, eyes closed until I could think.

Think.

I had to be smart. I could not afford to make a single mistake. My fever would only get worse now that I'd found her and couldn't claim her. I had to be fucking patient.

Tomorrow, I promised him. Tomorrow we would find release. Tomorrow we would no longer be alone and the fire burning through our body would stop burning. Hurting.

The maid was mine. She just didn't know it yet.

3

Angela, Twenty-Four Hours Later

"I'M TELLING YOU, Casey, I can't do it." I'd been hiding in the laundry room for ten minutes at least, my cell phone making my palm sweat. The phone battery made me hot. Plus the heat from the dryers. It was not the thought of going to that hot hunk of an alien's suite again, even if it was to clean his toilet bowl.

OMG. I seriously could not do it.

Casey, my best friend in the world since middle school, would normally be in town offering me stellar advice. Instead he was in Paris at some stupid fashion conference looking at shoes and handbags and clothes I hadn't been able to fit into since about third grade. I hated him and his posh job. *Paris.* While I stood in the bowels of a hotel, the humidity making my hair frizz.

"Listen to me, girlfriend," he countered. "You are going

to march your smoking-hot black ass onto that elevator, go to the top floor, and clean that man's room like a professional."

I rolled my eyes even though he couldn't see me from across a fricking ocean. "He's not a man."

Casey's very appreciative male laughter made me feel bad for every gay man within a hundred-mile radius of my best friend. "That is *not* what you told me last night. Oh, no. You said his cock was the size of a—"

"Don't!" I rubbed the sticky hair away from my face and sighed. "Don't remind me." Like I needed reminding. I'd thought of little else since I'd run from him yesterday. Him being an alien named Braun who was here, on Earth, to find the perfect woman on the *Bachelor Beast* television show. The one sexy alien every woman on the planet fantasized about.

Well, I'd also thought of his chest. His lips. Those muscled thighs.

"He probably won't even remember you, right?" he asked, the crackle of the line reminding me that it was amazing I could talk to my BFF thousands of miles away, but it made me realize that Braun had come from a planet millions of miles away. Millions. Of. Miles.

"That's what you told me last night," he added.

I couldn't help but roll my eyes. "After I told you he chased me down the hall."

Casey laughed. "Naked, too. You said you wanted to— what did you say again? Hmmm? Lick him all over? Ride him like a cowgirl?"

I face-palmed even though no one could see me. "Shut up, Casey. Don't remind me." Two glasses of wine, Oscar purring in my lap, and I'd admitted things to my best friend I shouldn't have.

"Woman, you wanted him. You never talked about Kevin like that. So why did you run? Have I taught you nothing? If a man you want to lick all over is chasing you, naked, you should stop and find out if he'll let you do it."

"No. I shouldn't." What a disaster. "At least I wasn't fired," I admitted. I'd been waiting all day yesterday after my shift was over for my boss to get in touch and tell me I'd been canned. No call had come, so I'd shown up this morning. Afraid. But no one had said anything nor taken me off the twelfth floor, so I'd gotten to work.

"You didn't do anything wrong," Casey prompted.

"I acted like an idiot and panicked. And ogled. I'm not supposed to drool over the guests." That was why I was nervous as hell now. Braun was the most beautiful creation I'd ever seen. And that was saying something, because I appreciated beauty in all forms. Especially *his*.

The two dozen gorgeous women lurking around the hallways who were always trying to catch him outside of his room were each stunning in their own way. Unique. Truly beautiful.

I'd delivered them a fine prize. Braun, naked and a long, long walk back to his suite. We might have been alone when I'd first bolted from his room, but I'd seen how the ladies had come from their rooms when he'd shouted, and gathered behind him, waiting to pounce as the elevator doors slid closed.

And when I'd seen Priscilla's hand slip around his biceps like she owned him?

I *still* wanted to scratch her eyes out of her pretty, perfect head.

"Well, you know what I think. I've told you a thousand times."

"Yes. I love you."

"Love you, too. Stop settling for assholes."

"Seems like they're all that's left." I was twenty-four, not thirteen. Most of my friends from high school had moved on. College. Trade school. Married. Whatever. They were living their life, and I was still trying to get mine started. Six years in nursing school had to be a record... and I still wasn't done.

I sighed the exact same moment my two-way radio went off.

"Angela. Are you finished with the Presidential Suite? I'm done on floor two. I can help if you need it."

"I'm okay. Thanks, Tina. Go on home." I spoke quietly into the radio, but Casey still heard every word.

"That's right, Ang. Go get him," Casey said. "Ogle the pants off the guy. Wait, his pants were already off!" He laughed. I didn't. "I want details when I get back in town next week."

"Shut up. You're such a player."

"You should be, too. It's more fun, especially when they're droolworthy."

"Whatever. Bring me amazing French shoes!" I reminded him before he hung up.

I slid the cell phone back into my pocket. Just like the ladies here to take their shot at winning Braun's heart—whose rooms I also cleaned this week—Casey was beautiful, sensual, and the exact opposite of me in terms of sexual aggression. If Casey saw a man he wanted, he went for it. He got turned down a lot, but that never stopped him from trying.

I could count on two fingers the number of men I'd slept with. Kevin had been fun, or so I'd thought. We were set up, friends of friends. He'd come across as a good guy. As the son of a state politician, he'd learned how to manipulate and lie. Fake shit like a pro. When he'd wanted to move in, I hadn't realized he'd been fired from his job and gambling to *try* and earn cash. It had been feast or famine with him, but he'd been too sly to let on. I let him live with me and realized too late what he was up to. For a guy with a daddy with really deep pockets—like super rich—Kevin had been stealing from me to pay his bookies. I'd kicked his ass to the curb... and all his belongings.

And then there had been Brandon, the sweet guy I'd met my freshman year of college. He was sweet, a real slow mover, and when he finally did make a move, he'd been a bit too quick on the orgasm side of things. At least when it came to his.

I'd figured we were young. That it took time to learn out our bodies. But that had been stupid thinking on my part. Kevin hadn't bothered with getting me off. I should have drawn him a map to my clit. I should have dumped him then, but stupidly I hadn't until I'd learned the hard way. The really *expensive* way that he was a dick. That he'd been hiding his habit, and me, from Daddy. I sighed, letting go of my angst with that asshole.

Unable to delay the inevitable another minute without literally risking my job, I pushed my cart onto the service elevator and made my way to the VIP floor and Braun's door.

I knocked three times.

"Housekeeping!"

Silence. Again.

The breath I hadn't realized I'd been holding escaped in a loud sigh. *Thank God.*

I knocked again and announced myself once more, just in case. When still no one answered, I used my key and entered the room. As usual, I left the cart in the hallway.

"Housekeeping!" I called again, not wanting a repeat of yesterday. Okay, maybe I did, but I was afraid I'd run again and make a fool of myself a second time. Once was enough.

When there was no answer, I went to the same bedroom, but this time I stuck my head in first. Empty. I tiptoed—like an idiot—to the bathroom door and peeked in there as well.

I sighed. Why was my heart beating out of my chest? Why did my skin prickle with disappointment? He wasn't here. I'd been avoiding him, but I was sad he wasn't around.

I was an idiot. And a hot mess.

I still had my job, so that meant I had to clean the suite. The thankfully *empty* suite.

When I went to collect my supplies, the suite door was closed. I gasped.

With his back to the door, blocking my exit, was Braun.

The alien.

The cyborg.

The sexiest fucking man I'd ever seen.

He looked bored, arms crossed over his chest—which, unfortunately, was covered with a tight T-shirt. The shirt matched the honey-brown color of his hair. He had golden eyes that would have looked unusual, even without the odd circle of silver I could just make out around his irises. And he was tall. Taller than I remembered even from the day before. The ceilings in this suite were just a few inches above his head.

Heaven help him, he'd have to duck to walk around without banging his skull on the light fixtures.

"Tell me your name."

Well, that wasn't what I had been expecting, and his order irritated me, especially since he was blocking my exit. I clenched my hands into fists, then flexed them. "I don't think so. I'll be going. Please call down to the front desk when you are ready to have your room serviced."

He didn't budge. Not. One. Inch. He didn't even blink, his golden eyes focused on me like twin lasers. I should be afraid, a guest not allowing me to leave a suite. I wasn't. Not with him.

"Please, female, I would be honored if you would deign to share your name with me."

I frowned. I hadn't heard anyone speak in such a formally polite way before. "Where did you learn to speak English?"

He was an alien from another planet. Last night I'd spent hours wondering how he had spoken to me. I'd heard about the NPUs that a bride received when she was matched so that on their new planet, she could understand her mate and any other language in the universe. But just because she could understand what she was hearing didn't mean she could speak the alien's language.

"To be eligible for the trip to Earth to find a mate, we must study and learn your language on The Colony," he replied.

"Do they make you take a test?"

"Of course. Have I misspoken?"

He looked genuinely upset at the idea, so I shook my head. "No. Your English is perfect."

"Your name. Please."

I'd shown him my name tag the day before, but it was possible they didn't have such things in space.

I had no hope of resisting him, not really. Not when he was being a gentleman. "Angela. Angela Kaur. My mom was born in Alabama, and my dad's from India. He's an engineer." Overshare much? Like a dam had broken, I kept going. Babbling. "And you're Braun, here for the *Bachelor Beast* show. Why did you chase me down the hallway yesterday? Why did you roar? And did you *see* all the women just waiting to sink their claws into you? The show hasn't even started yet, and they're circling you like beauty pageant vultures. How many followed you back to your room?"

It had to be pheromones, right? His. Making me babble and stare and *want*. And sounding like a jealous wench.

Stop. Talking.

His grin made my heart skip a beat. Holy crap, that smile was ruthless. It changed him from a formidable, possibly dangerous alien to... climb-him-like-a-monkey hot. "All of them."

"All of them?" Shit. I'd been joking. Mostly. I'd never felt so pea green with envy before. I hated every one of those bimbos and their fancy hair products.

"Were you jealous?" he asked.

Shit. What was the right answer here? The truth? The truth was hell yes, but I remained quiet and he kept talking.

"Do you know what I wished for?" His voice wasn't any softer, but it had gone quiet. As if he were sharing a secret even though we were completely, totally alone.

I shook my head as he moved away from the door and toward me. Slowly. Like I was a jumpy alley cat ready to bolt. I held myself still and swallowed. The closer he got, the more I had to tip my head back.

"You. I waited for you to come back." He reached up and touched the dark locks surrounding my face, rubbed the strands between his fingertips. "I called the front desk to ask for your name."

"You... you did?"

"Yes. They refused to give me your comm information or tell me where you live." His fingertips traced the arch of my brow before sliding down the side of my cheek. Goose bumps broke out along my skin. "All I could do was wait."

"Wait?"

"And hope."

"For what?" None of this was making sense.

"For this."

I should have taken a step back, excused myself from the room and gone about my business.

Consorting with guests would get me fired.

Letting one of them place his hands on my face and lean down like he was going to kiss me? That was definitely *consorting.* Worse, I *needed* this job. I'd just moved into my own apartment, and I was still helping my parents pay for the new experimental treatment Gramps was getting. He was doing great, seemed to be on the road to full remission. But that shit was expensive, and insurance didn't cover all of it. If I got fired, I'd never finish nursing school, and that was the gateway to a career and a good salary. And the only thing I hated more than cleaning toilets was looking for a new job.

No. I couldn't—

His thumb stroked my cheek, and I lost the ability to think. I wanted those hands *all over* me. All over. Every inch. He was huge. Powerful, yet his touch was beyond gentle, as if he was trying very hard to be careful. His chest was twice the width of a normal man's, and everything about him screamed *power*. Safety. Comfort.

Pleasure.

Shit. He was holding perfectly still, staring into my eyes as I fought this internal war with myself. If he'd moved at all, said anything, I probably would have bolted like a rabbit. Instead I stared back. And wanted more.

"What... what are you doing?"

His face hovered so close I was drowning in those gold and silver eyes. "Isn't it obvious? I'm going to kiss you, Angela Kaur of Earth."

Holy shit.

"Why?" Confusion was a living, breathing thing inside me. Why me? I was a maid. Poor. I had a hint of mascara on, but nothing else. My clothes were a two-day-dirty maid's uniform—and if I was careful, I could stretch it to three before hitting the laundromat. The most confusing factor? He had two dozen gorgeous, eager, elegant, perfect women ready to give him anything he wanted the second he stepped out of this room. Clothed or naked.

"Because you are beautiful and perfectly curved and you smell like—"

The way the words rushed out of his chest made my knees go weak. "Like what?" I desperately wanted to know *exactly* what he was going to say.

"Mine."

My heart skipped a beat. "You weren't kidding about the language classes, were you?"

"May I kiss you, female? Touch you? I need to touch you." His voice had taken on a fascinating timbre, almost like a growl, and he was breathing hard, the pulse at the base of his throat thundering away like a drum just beneath the skin. He wasn't lying. He wanted me.

Me!

Which was insane. But his touch, his gaze. I'd watched the video of Warlord Wulf taking out a cameraman to get to his woman. Braun wasn't acting *that* crazy, like knock down sets and growl, but he was intense. The longer I stood so close to him, the heat of his body enveloping me like a promise, the more turned on I became.

"Um..." *Yeah, real smooth.*

"You may kiss me, if you prefer." He inched closer until all I had to do to claim his lips was go up on my toes. Just barely.

Good God, this guy was lethal. Panty-melting, lose-your-damn-mind-and-give-him-anything-he-wants lethal.

And what did I want? Stupid, foolish, romantic me wanted that kiss. And more. A lot more.

Enough to get fired for it?

Yes. Turned out the answer to the question was yes. Hell yes. An I-want-him-naked yes. Casey wasn't wrong. I should *get some.*

My insecurities popped up to question everything, though. "Wait. You've got all the contestants. They're gorgeous."

"So are you."

"I'm a maid."

"You are honorably employed."

I'd never thought of it that way before.

"They're literally here for you."

"Who?"

"The contestants," I said, my frustration mounting.

"I have no desire for any of them. My language skills

must be poor if you still don't understand. My cock was hard for you yesterday as it is today."

I glanced down between us. Even though he was fully clothed—this time—I couldn't miss the thick outline of his *interest* in me.

My pussy clenched thinking of that thing fitting. Women across the world would bitch-slap me if I didn't shut up and take a beast for a ride.

"Okay." Once I made a decision, it was done. Finished. I didn't have time to second-guess my life.

Reaching up, I wrapped my arms around his head, dug my fingers into that gorgeous, honey-brown hair the way I'd wanted to since the first time I saw his photograph on a promotional graphic, and pulled him down to me.

Our lips met, and I could tell he was holding back. If I was going to get fired for this, that simply would not do. I wanted kissing and hot, up-against-the-wall, blow-my-mind sex. There was no way a condom was going to fit on Braun. I'd seen how big he was, knew that even the magnum size wasn't going to work. Fortunately I was on birth control. It wasn't like I was going to get pregnant with an alien baby. And I *wanted him.*

I wanted skin-on-skin action. I wanted to feel those muscles crushing my aching breasts. I wanted his hands all over every inch of skin. And I wanted his hard body buried deep.

I stepped back, breaking the somewhat chaste kiss. He groaned but let me go, his eyes going wide as I began to unbutton my uniform.

"What are you doing, female?"

"I want you, and I think you want me. And since everyone thinks I'm in here cleaning, this might be our only chance—" I let the thought hang in the air as I kicked off my shoes and tossed my uniform shirt across the arm of a chair. I was standing in my pants and bra, wondering if I'd just made a huge—HUGE—mistake when Braun dropped to one knee, his head down. One hand clawed at the carpeting; the other was in a fist at his side.

He moaned like he was in pain. Serious, terrible pain.

While he was kneeling before me, our heads were the same height. "Are you okay?"

"I cannot control him much longer."

"Who?" I looked around the room. What was he talking about? "Do you want me to go? I'm so sorry."

I reached for my shirt, freaking out at how I'd messed up. Again.

"No!" The barked command made me jump. When Braun lifted his face, I gasped. His jaw was wider, his face taking on a primitive structure that was still gorgeous, but more... just more. Thicker bones. Intense eyes. He looked like a wilder version of himself.

Then I knew. I'd seen that happen to Wulf on the show when he chased Olivia. "Your beast? Are you talking about your beast?"

"Yes." The word was not really a word. More a grumble of sounds that I could just make out.

"Will he hurt me if you let him out?"

"He will take what you offer, female."

"So, the beast likes sex. Will he hurt me, though?"

I had no idea what to do in this situation. Alien sex was not like wham-bam-thank-you-ma'am Earth-guy sex. Braun had a beast in him, and the beast wanted out. It wanted me.

That brought Braun up short, his body snapping to attention. "Never."

The vehemence of that statement made my pussy spasm with want. Holy shit. I dropped my shirt onto the floor. If this sexy beast man wanted me—me—instead of the parade of perfect women stalking him just outside this room, who was I to deny him or myself?

Wouldn't Casey be proud?

The thought made me smile, and I put my hands on my hips, my bright pink, lacy bra like a neon sign directing this man—alien—where I welcomed some attention. Man. Alien. Beast.

Whatever. I wanted him.

"Then let him out."

FOUR WORDS and this female made me come undone.

The beast within took over, and I had no chance to control him. For years I had held him in check, fought the mating fever back with cold logic, patience and pure will.

Now, because of what she'd said, he was hers. He would obey her. She was mine.

"Mine." I stood and watched Angela's dark eyes widen as I walked toward her, my beast breaking free, my body changing with every step.

With my last ounce of control I stopped before her, drew her scent into my lungs, my cock so hard I feared it might burst. But the agony was a welcome one. She was here. My mate.

My beast had chosen, and she was stunning.

Her hair was nearly black, not colorless like deep space but the rich darkness of human coffee. I lifted a hand to her shoulder and stroked her from collarbone to elbow, enjoying the soft slide of her skin. Her face had been even softer, and a low rumble of pleasure slipped from my beast's throat as I petted this female who stood before me, unafraid.

Her courage made me want her more. This female— Angela—was mine. I would kill to protect her. Do everything in my power to see to her happiness. Her pleasure. My beast had chosen, and so far, the male within was in full agreement.

I was also still in control, if barely.

Moving forward, I dropped to my knees directly before her, determined to feast on her breasts. The bright pink underthing she wore was tantalizing—and in my way.

"Off."

She moved her hands behind her back, which thrust her breasts forward. I buried my nose between them, eager to taste her skin, drown in her scent. I was not disappointed. The scent of something sweet—perhaps earthly flowers— and spice and female filled my head, and I had to growl at the beast to bring him back to heel.

I wanted this too, and that hulking bastard was just going to have to wait his turn. Her skin was the softest thing I'd ever felt, her curves ample to fill my hands.

The pink fabric dropped away, and I feasted on her nipples, pulling one then the other into my mouth as she buried her hands in my hair. She pulled and the beast fought me, hard.

"Do not move, female. I will lose control." The scent of her pussy flooding with wet welcome made me growl even louder, the sound nearly a roar. And again, another surge of musk and heat and female from her core. Hot, wet pussy driving the beast mad.

If I'd thought the threat would frighten her, I was mistaken. She laughed. Actually laughed.

"I'm not scared," she said as she tugged at my hair. "But you better keep that noise down or everyone in the hotel will know what we're doing in here."

"Yes." I wanted them to know this female was mine. My mate. My female. Mine.

"Yes, what? You want their noses in our business?"

"Yes."

She laughed again and pulled my face from her breasts. She leaned forward, her lips touching mine as she spoke. "Well, I like my privacy. So please don't be crazy loud, okay?"

The beast chose to respond with a low, rumbling growl, which made her smile as she pressed her lips to mine. She kissed me, and I was so shocked that this female was mine, that I had found her, that I could barely move as reality shifted.

I lifted my hands to her legs to learn the curve of her hips. I pushed her pants down until I came into contact with the small piece of fabric preventing me from reaching her core. Unacceptable.

With one tug, the irritating garment was gone and beneath my palms were the soft, full curves of her ass.

I devoured her now, her mouth mine. Slipping my fingers to her center, I dipped them just inside her pussy and found her hot. Wet. Ready.

The beast would not be denied.

Tearing myself from her kiss, I stood, reached for a chair

with fully padded armrests and placed it on top of the bed so I could have what I wanted. Her pussy. Hot. Wet. A feast.

This hotel was made for humans, not Atlan beasts. I'd have to make modifications to get what I wanted... her pussy on my mouth. Now.

She gasped when I lifted her, her hands flying to my shoulders as I placed her on her back in the chair, then worked off the rest of her clothes so she was completely bare. With the chair on the bed, she was at the right height for me. My beast was fully in charge now, which meant I could not say much.

Reaching for her legs, I splayed them wide, her pussy open and waiting before us.

"Stay."

The command—and it was a command—made Angela smile. Relaxing a little, I let my beast have what he wanted. Fuck that, what we both wanted. Our mouth on her. Tasting. Making her scream.

He was not gentle with her, and it was hard to fight him when her first moan of pleasure reached my ears. More wet heat. She threw her head back and held her knees wide on the chair. One finger in her pussy, I sucked and licked, playing with her sensitive flesh until I found the spot that drove her wild.

That drove me insane. That made me blissfully happy. That made me think... *finally.*

Her cries, however, were reserved, as if she were saving her pleasure for me and me alone. I discovered that as much as I loved that, the beast wanted more. He wanted her to lose control. Scream. Spasm all over his fingers as he sucked her wet flesh into his mouth.

I raised my free hand to pluck her nipple, squeeze and knead her breast as I finger fucked her with my other hand. I would not be denied.

She was panting now, her hands flying everywhere as if looking for something to hold on to. My beast did not like that.

"Me. Hands on me."

The deepness of my voice made her shudder, but she obeyed, burying her hands in my hair. Pulling. Hard.

The beast loved it. So did I.

Growling into her pussy, I worked her without mercy until she arched her back and cried out. Came all over my mouth and fingers. Fuck, yes. I'd satisfied my mate. I'd do so again and again before I was done with her. This time.

When she was panting and her body relaxed, I did it again. Possessive and cocky in our prowess. This time when she came, her pussy pulsing all over my fingers, I stood to my full height and opened my pants, settled my cock at her entrance and worked my way inside her body. The wet glide of her pulsating core made me groan, and her ass came up off the chair, her legs kicking into the air as I thrust deep.

"Mine." I thrust forward, buried himself in her honeyed, hot depths.

She whimpered and I fought my way to the surface, ready to battle the beast if he was too rough for her. I was big, and she was so small. I'd said I would never hurt her, and I would not do so now.

Then her legs wrapped around my hips and she shifted beneath me, took my cock deeper.

"God. You're huge, but yes. So good."

That was all I needed to hear. The beast took over,

rocking into her hard and fast. The chair threatened to tip over, so I reached for its arms, used the spring of the bed to rock Angela's body forward and backward, on and off my cock.

I fucked her. Claimed her. Buried my cock and my soul in her body. She was mine, the female I had given up hope of finding. Her breasts rocked back and forth, the dark nipples making me hungry for more. I would fuck her. Fill her with my seed. And then I would kiss every inch of her soft, brown flesh. I could learn every place she liked to be stroked, kissed, adored. And then I would fuck her again.

And again.

And again.

Until the torment I'd carried, the mating fever and the agony of its fire tearing through flesh and bone and mind was forgotten. A memory tamed by the female riding my cock.

Her head thrashed from side to side, and I knew she was close to another release. I wanted to feel her pussy spasm and squeeze my cock. I wanted to know I was buried deep when she screamed in pleasure.

I thrust and held, moving one hand from the chair to find her sensitive clit.

Stroking and rubbing, I quickly discovered exactly what she liked, her keening cry rising like a wild animal's call to her mate.

My beast answered, was ready. Her body pulsed, shuddered, her pussy rippling around my cock, milking me of my seed as I came inside her with a bellow of my own.

I could not move when it was over. Did not want to move. Neither did the beast. I stayed hunched over the chair, her body beneath me, her pussy around my cock for long minutes. Until I regained control. Until the threat of tears of satisfaction, resolution, and completion was gone.

She was mine. Gods be damned, I had nearly given up hope.

She was mine and she was beautiful. Passionate. Perfect.

ngela

REALITY CAME CRASHING BACK. I'd had sex—epic sex—with a guest. Not just any guest, but an alien. An alien so famous he was known across the globe as the latest bachelor beast. God, it had been good. No, amazing. Incredible. Not just the first time when he'd set me up high on a chair on the bed, but when he'd lifted me, ditched the chair, and took me once more. Then a third time. Any guy I knew would need time to recover. It was as if Braun could go all day.

My pussy was now spoiled by an alien lover, and I had no idea what I was going to do for the rest of my life. I was sore because he was big. I was sated because he was skilled.

I glanced at Braun, who was sprawled across the bed on the angle, the only way his large body wouldn't hang off the edge. The sheets and blankets were on the floor, pillows flung in different directions. It was clear what had been going on.

It hadn't been me cleaning the suite.

Which wasn't going to happen. Glancing at the bedside clock, I saw I'd been in here almost ninety minutes, which was reasonable if the suite was a mess. It hadn't been before I came in, but now a lamp was on the floor, the shade bent. The bed even fell at a slant, meaning Braun had broken the box spring with one of his hard thrusts. I'd been too well pleasured to even notice.

I couldn't help but grin.

I'd had sex so hot we'd trashed a hotel room. I wasn't that kind of girl.

Well, now I was. I could totally live with that. Live with the memory of what we'd just done. I wasn't going to think about Braun having headboard-banging sex with the woman he ultimately chose and put his mating cuffs on, but I refused to ruin the post-orgasm feelings I was having now with those miserable thoughts.

Sliding off the bed, I went in search of my uniform.

"Where are you going?" Braun asked. He didn't move, but his gaze followed me around the room.

"I have to work."

"How much work do you perform each day?"

I found my panties, realized they'd been torn. I glanced at him, not mad at all. "I work full-time, which is eight hours a day, five days a week. But I do as much overtime as I can if I can make it fit in with school."

"You work too hard."

I shrugged and slipped my arms through the bra straps. "Bills don't pay themselves."

"You have more rooms to clean today?"

Grabbing my skirt, I sat on the edge of the bed to tug it on. Since my panties were ruined, so commando was my only option. "No. But I can't stay in here any longer. My cart's out in the hall, and people will talk."

"I do not care what others think."

I whipped my head around, my long hair hitting me in the face, and I tucked it behind my ear. "I do. I broke the rules doing this with you. I could be fired."

"Lose your job?" He sat up in bed as if he were ready to slay some dragons for me. "That will not happen."

I couldn't help but laugh at his vehemence. "It's not like my boss will think you'd want to sleep with me anyway."

His eyes narrowed with a speed that surprised me. He reached out and tugged me onto his lap and gave my covered butt a swat. I put my hand back. "Hey! What was that for?"

"I do not wish for you to speak about yourself in such a way."

He let me go, and I climbed from the bed to grab my uniform top. My butt stung a little, but I was also a lot turned on. I'd never been spanked before, but... wow.

"Fine. I have to return my cart and clock out. I mean, end my workday."

"Excellent. I will come with you."

I turned and stared at him. "What?"

"I have nothing to do," he admitted. "Chet Bosworth has something called pink eye, and we are delaying production."

I bit my lip to keep from laughing. "Seriously?"

"What is this ailment?"

"You really want to know?"

He nodded.

"Well, it's when you get a bacteria in your eye that makes

it pink and irritated. It's caused from... well, not washing your hands or touching someone who hasn't washed their hands after using the bathroom, and then rubbing your eye."

He stared at me as if he was trying to understand; then he grimaced.

I couldn't help but laugh again.

"That could be easily remedied with a ReGen wand."

I frowned. "What's that?"

"A device that heals bodily injuries."

God, that must be nice. "Yeah, well, there are worse things than pink eye a magic wand could heal."

"Earth is too primitive for such technology. As for Chet Bosworth's... infliction, I shall not be shaking anyone's hands on this planet," he vowed. "Because of his uncleanliness, I have free time. Days of it, since I've been interviewed several times and they are now doing the same with the female contestants. Angela Kaur of Earth, I wish to continue to spend time with you."

Exhilaration filled me at the prospect of him wanting to be with me. "It can't happen here in your room... or in the hotel, and I assume you can't leave the building."

He was silent for a moment. "You will get in trouble if you stay, correct?"

I nodded. I couldn't be seen coming and going from Braun's suite with him, on the clock or off.

"I will get in trouble if I leave the hotel, as you said," he repeated. "Then there is only one option. I will, as you humans call it, sneak out."

I laughed again. "You? Sneak out?"

It would be easier for an elephant to walk through the lobby unnoticed than a gorgeous, seven-foot alien.

He climbed from the bed and came over to me. Gloriously virile and naked. I couldn't help but stare. "Do you wish to spend the remainder of the day with me?"

A bubble of happiness filled my chest, and I tipped my chin back to smile at him. "Yes."

"Then we must come up with a way for me to sneak out."

I felt like a teenager trying to get a boy in my bedroom window without grown-ups finding out. In reverse.

"Oh! I have an idea." It wasn't great, but it could work. "Will you give me a few minutes?"

"Yes."

I turned and left the bedroom.

"Wait! Where are you going?" He rushed after me and stepped in front of the door before I could open it. "My beast is not happy with the idea of you leaving us."

"Tell your beast I have to trade carts, so I need to go to the basement."

A rumble came from his chest. His hands were clenched into fists atop his thighs, and they were shaking. "You will return?"

Instinct had me placing my hands over his wrists, and for some reason that calmed him. I had no idea why he was so concerned I wouldn't come back. It made me realize he wasn't just strong and sexy and dominant, but he was vulnerable, too. The fact that I had such a powerful effect on someone so huge melted my heart just a little bit. No, a lot. My heart melted into a puddle, and I found myself wanting to take care of him.

Me. Which was ridiculous, because he was pure muscle and the top of my head barely reached his chest, but somehow I had power over this man—alien—the power to make him happy. At least for today.

"Yes. I give you my word. I will return." Before I left the suite, I looked myself over, made sure I didn't appear as if I'd been ravaged by an alien. I took a deep breath and forced the smile I couldn't prevent from tugging at my lips to drop. Realizing I couldn't leave empty-handed after supposedly working for an hour, I went over to one of the trash cans and grabbed the plastic bag and took it with me into the hall.

The door slipped shut behind me, and I tucked the trash into the cart. A quick glance down the hall showed it was empty. My hands were shaky, as if I'd just robbed a bank instead of fucking an alien. I pushed the cart to the service elevator and tried my best to look completely innocent and severe at the same time. I made the trip to the basement without any issue, clocked out and tracked down an empty laundry cart.

The lower levels of the hotel were busy at all times of the day. Employees were everywhere since the two basement floors housed everything from housekeeping to food service. When I grabbed a stack of clean blankets from a shelf and dropped them into the cart, no one paid me any attention.

Back on the VIP floor, I knocked on Braun's door again, calling out, "Housekeeping!" because that was what I was supposed to do. A woman waiting at the elevator looked my way, but the car arrived and she was gone before Braun opened the door. He'd gotten dressed while I was gone.

I pushed the cart in, and the door closed behind me. Before I had a chance to blink, Braun gently pressed me against the door and kissed me. *Kissed* was too basic a term for what his mouth was doing. More like devoured. I'd been gone maybe ten minutes, but he was practically ravenous for me. A rumble escaped his chest, and I felt it in mine.

When I could pull myself away, I stared up at him. "It's only been a few minutes."

He held me pressed to him, one hand at the small of my back, and the other he lifted to cup my cheek. "No, it has been a lifetime."

His heat surrounded me. His palm was an anchor that made me feel about a dozen different things all at once. Safe. Desired. Beautiful. Pursued. Protected. My entire body wanted to melt into him and the comfort and heat he offered. And then I'd want to get naked again, because his scent called me like nothing else ever had.

I was losing my mind. That had to be it. My mind. My good judgment. My willpower. My self-discipline. He was wrecking me, and I was enjoying it.

"I am in so much trouble here." I couldn't tear my gaze from his, not for a moment.

"Nothing will hurt you, Angela. Never again." Braun lowered his head, and this time when he kissed me, he killed me with tenderness. If I was broken china, he was the glue putting me back together and telling me I was still worthy and beautiful and perfect.

I started crying, for no damn good reason. None at all. I'd just never been held like that. Kissed like that.

Damn it.

Stepping back, I turned to discreetly wipe at my cheeks. "We should get going. You need to call down to the front desk and tell them you do not want to be disturbed under any circumstances."

"Why?"

"Trust me. You're a VIP guest. If you tell them you don't

want to be disturbed, not even pink-eye Chet will be able to come up to your room without a police escort."

"All right." He stared at me, his brows drawn together as if I'd confused him. But he stepped away to make the call. When he put the phone back on the cradle, he shook his head. "Human comm systems are primitive."

"It works. And that was perfect. Now let's go."

"This is how I shall sneak out?" he asked, tipping his head to the cart.

"You'll have to scrunch down."

I reached in and grabbed the blankets, waited for him to step into the cart. He did and he had to stoop so he didn't whack his head on the ceiling.

He gave me a heated gaze, then squatted down.

I laughed because he was so big he wasn't even below the top edge of the cart.

Glancing at me again, he narrowed his eyes, then somehow maneuvered himself—with a grunt of effort—so he was on his side, curled up in the tightest ball. I leaned over and looked down at him and had to wonder how big he'd been as a baby. Probably huge.

"I'm going to put these blankets over you," I said, gently laying them over him so he was covered. "I'll go as fast as I can, but we have to go down to the basement and into the parking garage. No peeking."

He grunted once more but said nothing.

I opened the door, cased the hallway. Grabbing the *Do Not Disturb* sign, I attached it to his door for good measure— the front desk would red light his room so no one disturbed him, but I couldn't guarantee good behavior from the contestants. That done, I pushed out the laundry cart and turned toward the service elevator even though there were two women at the other end of the hallway. This was the one time I was thankful for being invisible, for while they glanced my way, they didn't give me any of their attention.

I got back to work... sneaking a hot alien warlord out of the hotel.

————

MY APARTMENT BUILDING was three stories tall, built of brick back in the days when things were made to withstand a bomb blast. That meant it was ugly, but I didn't have to hear my neighbor's TV either. I lived on the top floor, and my small deck faced the parking lot in the back.

"This is me," I said, stepping inside and holding the door for him.

He ducked his head and entered my small living room. I didn't have much money after helping pay for Gramps's medications. Some went to my college classes, but was sometimes short and couldn't take more than one class in a semester. Anything left over covered rent and food. There wasn't any time between working at the hotel full-time and school for anything fun, which was good since there weren't pennies to rub together for that.

Someday soon I'd be in a better setup. There were tons of nursing jobs, so I was eager for that larger paycheck... and working in a field that I found fulfilling.

He glanced around, and I tried to imagine how he saw my place. The living room had Gramps's old couch, the one he'd passed down to me when he'd downsized into an apartment in an elderly community where they took care of his yard and hosted social gatherings at the community clubhouse. I'd tossed a blanket over it to cover the frayed and worn cushions, but it was comfortable as hell. I used the coffee table as my eating spot and put a desk where a dining set should normally go. It had my ancient computer on it and my textbooks and notebooks. The kitchen wasn't big enough for me to stand in with Braun, and my bed was a twin so he better not want to take a nap. My bathroom had an avocado-green tub, toilet, and sink, so I had no doubt that would destroy any thought Braun might have about humans being advanced.

"It is small like you," he said, then was distracted as Oscar weaved in and out of his legs.

My cat was a small fluffy white Persian with green eyes and a bad attitude. He'd been so adorably fierce as a kitten when I brought him home, I'd named him Oscar. As in *the Grouch.*

The name stuck—and boy was it fitting. That cat hated my ex, Kevin. Although maybe Oscar had known something I hadn't and I should have paid more attention to his attitude toward the loser. Oscar tolerated the neighbor, but only because she tossed treats to him on the deck every morning.

"What is that creature?" He raised his hands in front of him as if afraid.

I went over to him, picked up Oscar, and tucked him in my arms. When I stroked his furry head, he purred. I glanced up at Braun. "He sounds like you."

"I do not rumble like that," he countered as if offended.

I thrust Oscar at him. "Here."

He didn't have a choice but to take the animal, and I stepped back, wanting to see how he handled a cute little cat.

Braun pet Oscar just as I had, the cat closing his eyes in

happiness. A louder purr came from him. Braun smiled. "This is a pet?"

"Yes. A cat. They come in all different colors. Well, some different colors. There aren't any blue or red cats or anything like that." I added all that just in case I gave him the impression there was a feline fur rainbow.

He went over to my couch and sat down, the old frame groaning slightly in protest, and continued to stroke the cat. God, he looked... cute with the little beastie in his arms. I didn't dare say that to him.

I stared, a little besotted by the giant beast and my fluffy white kitty. Every time I thought one way about him, he changed my opinion. He was possessive and bossy and yet gentle and sweet.

He looked up at me. "Stop looking at me that way."

I blinked, then frowned. "What way?"

He pointed and circled a finger. "That way. Like you want to lick me or jump me or..."

The grin was impossible to restrain. "I'm jealous of my cat."

A pale brow winged up. He glanced at the cat content in his arms, then back at me. "Why would you be jealous of a pet?"

"Because I want to be petted, too."

His eyes narrowed and heated. He leaned forward, set the cat on the floor, then leaned back. Curled his finger and beckoned me closer.

I closed the distance between us, moving to stand between his parted legs. Because he was so tall, we were pretty much eye level.

"You do purr when I pet you just right," he murmured, setting his hands on my hips. "Scream, too."

My cheeks went hot at the blatant reminder of how wild I'd been with him. Hell, he'd set a freaking chair on the bed so he could fuck me just right. I wasn't the only one who'd gone a little wild.

"Are you sore?" he asked, his pale eyes meeting mine.

I *was* a little. His cock was impressive and it had been a while. I was sore, but still...it didn't matter. I wanted him again. "Not enough to keep from having you again."

"You, having me?" I saw laughter in his eyes, as if he found me funny. Yeah, my statement was a little strange. Me, the five-foot nothing telling an Atlan I was going to *have him again.*

I was feeling bold though. I knew he wanted me. He was in my apartment, not at the hotel. There was no one to worry about. No job to lose here.

He didn't judge me. He didn't look at my thighs and ask why they rubbed together. He didn't comment on the size of my butt or the more-than-a-handful boobs. He'd seen *all* of me and had been... reverent. Completely unlike Earth guys. So different from Kevin.

Stop it. No. No thinking about Kevin when I had an eager alien ready to go on my couch.

For the second time in a few hours, I tugged off my shirt and bra. Braun watched, stared. Practically drooled. He cupped my breasts, and my eyes fell closed, head dropped back.

"They fill my hands."

Hmm, they did. Maybe they were so big because they were meant for Braun. I had no idea how long he worked them, cupping, kneading, tugging on the nipples. It was when he stopped that I moaned and glanced at him.

"Get that beast out of your pants, big guy." His eyes

widened as I pushed down my pants and toed off my sneakers. "Now."

He did as told, lifting his hips just enough to get his
pants down and his cock out.

I'd never been so forward before, so eager to be fucked.
And even though there was an Atlan on my couch, I was the
aggressor here. Or, more realistically, he was *letting* me be
the one in charge, because he could hurt me. Easily.
Without even trying.

Setting my hand on his arm for balance, I climbed onto
his lap, placing my knees on either side of his hips. He was
almost too big for this to work, but I stayed up on my knees
and kissed him. His cock was pressed into my belly, hard
and long and thick between us.

His hands slid down my back and then cupped my ass.

He pulled back and kissed along my jaw. "Are you wet? I
will not hurt you no matter how eager you are."

God, he was a good kisser. He was so warm, like a huge
furnace. My nipples were hard, my pussy aching for him. I
broke the kiss, glanced down between us. I couldn't lift up
any higher to get his cock aligned with my pussy. My legs
were just too short.

"Lift me up. I'm ready. I'm wet," I said, frustrated. He
chuckled and ran his finger up and down my slit. He
growled and I assumed that was his beast, satisfied.

"Fuck, mate. You are dripping for me."

"I'm dripping *from* you. From earlier. Now shut up and
fuck me."

I was so turned on, so crazed with need, I was practically
clawing at his arms.

"Your desire is my command." Braun lifted me by the

waist so that I hovered over him, then lowered me down, opening me up around his cock as he filled me.

"Oh my God," I moaned, squirming to take him all. This position was different, and he went so deep.

He growled again, the feel of it rumbling from his chest.

"Mine," he said.

"Yes. Yes!"

I wiggled my hips, tried to lift up, but I only managed to pull off him about an inch. His thighs were just too big. I was too small. This wasn't going to work. I couldn't even ride him. Instead I was impaled on him and couldn't do anything about it.

"Braun," I moaned. "Please."

"So needy. Greedy," he said, cupping my hips again and lifting me up, dropping me down.

"Yes."

He did it again.

"Oh."

And again.

"Oh my God."

"You were made for me, Angela Kaur." He lifted and lowered me at a consistent pace. Slow up, hard drop so he slid deep. He lifted his hips and thrust, filling me completely. I wasn't sure if what he said was true. I was too small and we had to make it work. The chair on the bed. I couldn't ride him like I wanted, but God, this felt so good.

"I want no other. You are mine. My mate."

He kept talking as we fucked, but I tuned out the words. I was too lost in my pleasure, what he was giving me, what I was taking. I couldn't handle any more pleasure. It was almost too much. I was about to come, and come so hard I was thankful for the bunker-like qualities of my apartment. No one would think I was being murdered as I screamed.

Reaching between us, I rubbed my clit. Braun slowed to watch, to see what I was doing.

"Yes, mate," he approved, lifting me faster and dropping me with more intent, as if to prove he could get me off.

"Braun," I panted. "Please." I was so close, but he was almost too much. My brain was starting to kick back in as I imagined what I must look like bouncing on his lap like a nymphomaniac, begging for more.

He grunted, then got busy, as if it was his mission to make me have an orgasm. More than one.

It worked. He increased the pace, his rumbling growl making my pussy flutter and my skin chill. My brain shut down completely, and I felt crazed. Like I would explode into little pieces without his heat and cock and hands anchoring me to reality.

What guy ever did that? Not just the first time I cried out his name and came all over his cock, but the second time when I whimpered through the rolling pleasure, or the third time when he thrust hard and came on a growl, pushing me once again so I collapsed in a boneless heap against his huge chest.

I was lulled by the beating of his heart, the slide of his hand up and down my sweaty back.

I may have even passed out for a bit, but I remembered what he'd said. He'd called me *mate*.

Had he meant it? Was I the one he'd been seeking? The one to wear his cuffs?

I had no idea, but if the test was based on sexual compatibility, I'd say he might just be right.

I had no idea how I'd be able to be with any other guy ever again.

I wanted Braun. I wanted his cock. Hell, I wanted his heart because mine was already on the way to being his.

Curling into him, I didn't protest when he carried me to bed, stripped me naked and held me, his hands stroking my back for what felt like hours of bliss. I fell asleep to the sound of my Atlan and my cat, both purring.

*raun*

DAWN LIGHT FILTERED through the thin fabric covering Angela's bedroom windows, and I watched the shadows from them creep along the wall as daylight arrived. I had not slept. Instead I held the small female who lay sprawled across my chest and soothed my beast by touching her skin, rubbing my hands over her body with a contentment and peace I never had been able to imagine, no matter how often I'd thought of finding my mate.

She was soft and warm, and her scent surrounded me.

Angela was mine. The beast knew this to be true. But since I had kept him restrained, worried to allow him loose without the mating cuffs around mine and Angela's wrists, he paced inside me like a wild thing even as we rested.

Impatient. Angry. And growing stronger with each passing moment.

Soon I would not be able to control him. Angela's nearness was both blessing and curse. The beast knew she was ours, and at the same time he fought harder for freedom.

The beast needed to claim her, accept her dominion over us. She was now the only being in the universe standing between me and total madness, a killing rage... and execution.

The beast within didn't care about dying. He was not afraid of the prison cells on Atlan, nor fighting and destroying everything and everyone around him.

He only wanted one thing.

Her.

Yet until she had been claimed in the traditional Atlan way, with my cuffs about her wrists, he would not be satisfied.

The creature, Angela's pet, sat hunched on the small wooden table next to her bed. His green eyes focused on me in the dark as if he were a fierce hunter and I, his prey.

The cat, as she'd called him, looked ready to pounce, and he was no longer purring. I reached for him to stroke his white fluffy fur as I had done last night.

Oscar, my mate's beloved pet, lifted a paw and swiped at me with his tiny claws.

Little devil.

He hissed at me in the semidark.

Chuckling, I hissed back. "A bold one, I approve. You believe you are protecting our female." He wasn't mighty, but he was fierce.

The slow blink of his green eyes made me wonder if the tiny fluff ball actually understood what I was saying to him —or if he was contemplating attack. Both thoughts made me smile.

"What's going on?" Plastered to my side, Angela lifted her head to stare at her pet. "Oscar, stop it."

I ran my fingers through her hair, enjoying the texture of the springy curls. "Your pet is trying to protect you from a beast."

She set her chin on my chest as she grinned, then tipped her head to place a kiss on that spot. I thought my heart might explode while the beast roared inside me to break free. Even a gesture so simple could push me to the brink. I took a deep breath, tried to calm.

"He's such a pain." She reached her arm over me and touched her pet, stroking his face. Which, of course, the fluff ball allowed. From her. Not that I blamed him. I wanted Angela to stroke me as well.

She *had* done so the night before, and quite well, her hands wrapped around my cock bringing me to the edge of satisfaction, but I'd tugged her hands away and finished deep inside her, only after she'd come. Of course.

Staring at me like he was a king and I, a peasant not worthy to look upon him, Oscar stood on his four paws, jumped off the table and onto the bed, then walked across my chest to stare down into my face.

I frowned at the tiny beast. "What is he doing?"

She snuggled into my shoulder and giggled. "I think he likes you."

"Absolutely not." I lifted my hand to show her the scratches Oscar had given me just before she'd awoken. "He is a fierce attack pet, determined to defend you."

"What?" She pulled my hand down closer to her face for inspection. "No. I'm so sorry." She looked at Oscar, her eyelids narrowed. "Oscar. Bad kitty. You don't scratch Braun."

The cat turned from staring at me to looking down at her.

"He is unrepentant." I stated the obvious. The cat king was looking at Angela as if she, too, were a minor subject.

A smile had spread on my face when the small creature lowered its head and smashed his forehead into mine. "What?"

"Oscar. Don't headbutt our guest."

Oscar did it again, this time making a strange mewling noise.

"No, it's not breakfast time yet."

There was that slow, deliberate, *you-will-serve-me* look in Oscar's green eyes. He glanced from me to Angela, the mewling growing louder.

"No."

Irritated, Oscar settled into a ball on my chest and laid down like he owned me.

Angela laughed and removed herself from my arms as I held perfectly still, unsure what to do about the tiny ball of fur atop me. "See, told you he likes you."

I wasn't so sure.

Angela moved to her bathing room. "I'm going to take a shower. I have the day off—well, I'm free until six. I was supposed to meet my parents. But we don't have to if you don't want to go."

Her cheeks were turning a deep rose shade as I stared. My mate would become used to such attention. She was beautiful, and I would admire her.

"Well?"

"Yes?"

"What do you want to do?"

I was hers to command. I would go where she wished

and was surprised she requested an answer. I took in every inch of her and remembered how I'd learned her body intimately and thoroughly. "Keep you naked." My answer was one-hundred-percent honest, but she laughed, the sound making my chest ache in a new and uncomfortable manner.

Females were dangerous.

"Stop it." I heard the water spray begin, and she stuck her head around the open door. "Let's go to the beach. You need to get out. You can wear a hat. We'll disguise you as a basketball player. They're tall."

"I am not tall." In terms of an Atlan, I was average.

"You are. And please say yes. Have you been to the beach before?" She frowned for a moment. "I don't even know if they have beaches on Atlan. God, I know nothing about where you are from."

I would rectify that soon, but not now. I did not make that planet my home, but I wanted her to see it. To understand about me. She would learn the most about The Colony, where we would live.

"There is water, of course, but from what I've seen of images of Miami and Florida, it will be strikingly different. I look forward to you showing me."

She smiled then. "Good, we'll make a day of it, but I have something at six."

Oscar was making the purring sound again, so I held still, admiring my mate. "What happens at six?"

"I have class from six to nine."

"What type of class?"

"I'm in my last year of nursing school. I know what you're thinking, I'm too old to be in school."

I wasn't thinking that at all.

"You work many hours and attend schooling? Your time is full."

"Yeah. It's pretty brutal, but that's how it's got to be. It's taking forever because I had to help my parents and all that. But I'm almost done. Next semester I'll start my final round of clinicals and then I'll get my license." She turned back around, and I watched her perfectly round ass shake as she walked away.

The beast growled, and Oscar knew what was good for him. He jumped off my chest like I'd set his fluffy white tail on fire.

Angela's soft voice drifted to me in the bedroom, and I listened for a few moments, enjoying the sound of her happiness. She should be exhausted, and I should have given her more time to sleep than to fill her with my cock and make her scream. I would ensure she had a balance of both. I'd fuck her senseless, then let her rest.

I had never been this intimate with a female before, never known the small moments of pleasure or contentment, the true nature of a mate and the private moments spent bathing or sleeping or watching her laugh in my arms. Of thinking of her needs and concerns. It was my job to help carry her burdens. I was strong enough to do so.

I'd had lovers when I was younger, as all warlords in training did. The females on my world were eager to ride the cock of a warlord and hoped to be chosen. If the male survived the war and his time in the Coalition Fleet, he would be gifted with land and a home as well as more than enough wealth to support himself and a family for the rest of his life.

I had never returned to Atlan. I had been captured by the Hive, integrated, and somehow survived long enough to end up on The Colony. It might not be the place of my birth, but it was my home.

And now I'd found her. My true mate. The female capable of taming my beast and the mating fever raging in my blood.

I understood very little of what she'd said of class and clinicals, but I determined that I would find out more later. Medical training with the Coalition was rigorous and for the most intelligent, which meant my mate was not only honorable but brilliant. I would learn everything about her. *Everything.*

At the moment the only thing I could do was rise from the bed, follow her into her bathing chamber, and take her again. My cock was instantly hard at the idea, and my beast was in complete agreement.

There was a strange curtain separating her from me, and I slid it aside to find her body slick with soap. Everywhere. She held a spraying device in her hand and was trying to rinse the bubbles from her dark skin. Her eyes were closed, the steam rising from the water letting me know my mate liked the temperature hot.

"Allow me." I stepped into the small area and took the spraying device from her hands.

"Oh!"

I reached for the soap and used one hand to rinse her off as I cleansed my own body with the other. Less than two minutes later I lifted the spraying device back into its holder and turned to my mate.

"What are you doing?" she asked, eyeing me with the same needy gleam as I'd stared at her.

"You are beautiful." Lifting my hands, I cupped her

breasts. She swayed, one hand going to the tiles on the wall to maintain her balance.

That would not do. I did not want her worried about falling.

In one quick move I lifted her and placed her back to the wall, her shoulder and side under the spray so she would not become cold. Bending my knees, I lifted her up, higher and higher, and placed her thighs over my shoulders. My arms encircled her and cupped her back. I stared at the gorgeous pussy spread open before me. *Right. There.*

She startled. "What? Shit, don't drop me."

That worry caught my attention. "Never. I will allow nothing to harm you." I didn't wish for her to panic. My intention was the opposite, to relieve her of any and all worries and make her come. On my tongue so I could have her taste as we went to the beach.

Her eyes went soft, and she lifted her hands to bury them in my hair. "You're crazy!" She laughed. "What are you doing?"

"Tasting you." As if that hadn't been my obvious plan.

"But we just—"

I cut her off with my tongue pressing into her wet heat. Her hands dug into my hair, twisting and pulling to draw me closer, and my beast howled with delight, fighting to break free.

I held her in place and feasted, giving her no time to recover. No mercy. So much for letting her rest. I needed to touch and feel her, to satisfy her. She needed to be pleasured, to be taken care of.

She tasted so sweet, musky and feminine, but I tasted myself as well. I'd filled her with enough of my cum. It didn't bother me. Instead it made my balls ache to empty into her again. My beast was satisfied knowing she was marked as ours. Not yet claimed, but it was a close second.

When she shuddered, her pussy going into a flurry of spasms around my tongue, I lowered her body so our mouths met for a kiss. One soul-searing kiss, then lower until her pussy melted onto the top of my cock.

"Braun." She said my name—mine—and the beast demanded we fuck her. Hard. Up against the wall. Standing strong to protect our mate. Fuck, did I wish I had my cuffs. I could put them about her wrists now and make her mine.

But no, I'd have to get them later. I would not leave her now. Not needy and wet and eager. That didn't help me settle. In fact, it made my beast push to take her hard. Fast.

Because of this, there was no gentleness left in me, but Angela didn't seem to need gentle, not right now.

Her fingers clenched at my shoulders, the nails digging into my skin. "Hurry. I need you inside me."

Not one to argue, I thrust my cock up and into her hot pussy, shuddered at the pleasure that nearly brought me to my knees. I would never get enough of her. My cock would always be hard. I might be several feet taller and carry double her weight, but she held all the power. She had no idea the control she had over me. Her pussy might be impaled by my cock, but my life was in her hands.

"So good." My mate's hands were roaming, touching me everywhere she could reach, encouraging me to fuck her, fill her, claim her. "Braun!"

I would deny her nothing. Not today. Not ever.

I fucked her until she screamed again, until I could hold nothing back, then filled her with my seed. When it was over, I held her gently and washed every inch of her, more as an excuse to explore her curves than because either one of us was dirty.

When she was limp and drained and smiling, I turned off the water and wrapped her in the softest towel I could find. Then I kissed her. Again. Because I had to. Because I could. Because she was mine.

"Now, mate, the beach. My only request is that we have ice cream."

"Ice cream?" she asked.

"Yes. Besides that, you may take me anywhere you wish to go."

ngela

IT WAS HARD NOT to laugh at Braun as he was folded into my car. Even with the passenger seat back as far as it could go, he had to scrunch down so his head wouldn't hit, but then his knees were practically in his nose.

"We're almost there," I told him, driving down the main drag toward the nearest beach.

He only gave a grunt of reply.

It wasn't the weekend, so it wasn't too busy. While I usually drove with the music blasting, I turned it down so it wasn't too distracting. By the look on Braun's face when he'd first gotten into my car the other day, he wasn't really into Earth tunes.

My cell chimed, indicating a text.

"Will you get that?" I pointed to the center console where I'd set my phone. He'd said Earth was primitive in comparison to space, so I took a guess he could figure out my simple cell phone.

He picked it up, fumbled with it for a second. I put on my blinker and moved into the left turn lane and stopped, waiting for the light to change.

Angling the screen toward me, he said, "I do not know this animal."

"Shit," I muttered, looking at the picture. "That's Howard."

"That is the kind of animal? A Howard?"

I glanced at the stoplight and sighed with relief when it changed to green. Instead of turning onto the side street that went toward the beach, I did a U-turn to go back the direction we came. "That's an alligator that likes to wander around in my grandfather's backyard. Gramps named it Howard."

I pulled into a strip mall parking lot and put the car in park. I never used my cell and drove, and this was going to take a little work.

"This is not the beach." Braun swiveled his head left and right, trying to find the water.

"Yeah, sorry. I've got to make a call." I swiped a few times, then pressed my grandfather's name.

"Hello."

"Gramps, you need to go inside." Based on the photo he'd sent, it was obvious that he was in the backyard with Howard. I had no idea if Howard was a girl or boy alligator, but he'd come from the swamp up onto Gramps's backyard for a few years now.

"He's harmless."

"He's a wild animal."

Braun watched me as I spoke.

"He likes beef jerky."

"I bet he does," I muttered. What carnivore didn't like dried meat sticks?

My cell chimed, and I pulled it from my ear and slid my finger across the screen to read the text. My mother. I'd set up a group text between me, Gramps, and my parents so we could communicate easily. Gramps had no issue with texting or taking pictures and sharing them through his phone with the three of us. I hadn't seen a picture of Howard in a while. Usually Gramps would send an image of his dinner or a pretty sunrise or even a junk mail letter stating he'd won ten million dollars.

Gramps had sent his favorite alligator shot to the group chat, so I wasn't the only one who'd seen it.

MoM: *At the hardware store waiting for paint to be mixed. Get over there. Get your grandfather and that beef jerky away from Howard!*

I SIGHED, realizing that Mom had also dealt with this exact issue in the past and even knew about the snacks. I put the phone back to my ear. "Gramps, please go inside until he's gone."

"We're keeping each other company," he replied. "He missed me while I was gone."

My grandfather had been in the hospital for a few days, the chemo messing with him, but he'd been home a week now. I ran a hand over my face, flicked my gaze to Braun. "Want to see an alligator?"

His eyebrows went up.

"Are you with someone?" Gramps asked.

"Yes."

"I wish to see an alligator named Howard," Braun commented.

"Is that a man?" Gramps might have health problems, but hearing wasn't one of them.

I looked Braun over. Was he a man? He was male, that was for certain. I'd thoroughly confirmed that.

"Yes," I said, not getting into the ins and outs of Atlans over the phone.

"Will I get to meet him?"

I looked to Braun again. It was one thing to have a fling with a guy, alien. Man. Another entirely to take him to meet your family after knowing each other for two days. I didn't have much choice. Gramps had survived a war and was putting up a good fight against cancer. I didn't want him to go out being eaten by an alligator.

"In about fifteen minutes," I said.

"Great, pick up some more beef jerky on the way." Gramps ended the call, so I set my cell back in the console, but it chimed and I grabbed it back up to find another text.

MOM: *Please say you're on your way to deal with the alligator.*

I SIGHED and answered that I was going to take care of it.

"What bothers you?" Braun wondered as I typed the reply.

"Nothing," I said, not looking up. "It's my mother, and she saw the picture and is worried."

"You have a caring family."

My thumbs paused on my screen, and I glanced to Braun. Did he have family? I had no idea. He lived on The Colony though, and from what I'd heard, it was for fighters alone, not their families. Heck, I'd even heard it was because the guys who lived there were shunned by their own people. That just wasn't right.

"I do," I replied, hitting send. "I've reassured my mother we will take care of Howard and stop Gramps from feeding him any more beef jerky."

Braun nodded. "Excellent. I wish to see this creature and to meet your grandfather. And if this beef jerky is good, to try some."

Even with the windows down, it was hot in the car since we weren't moving. If I was overheated, then Braun had to be melting, although there wasn't even a drop of sweat on his brow.

I pulled back into traffic and tried to figure out the guy beside me. He liked cats. He wasn't afraid of family. He didn't complain about being wedged into my car. He wanted to eat something that was fed to an alligator. What was wrong with him? I spent the drive wondering, but by the time we pulled up in front of Gramps's house, I hadn't come up with anything.

Braun stood and stretched as I came around the car to join him. "What do I need to know?" he asked.

"Big teeth. Short legs. Runs fast."

His eyes widened in shock. "Your grandfather?"

I blinked, confused, then laughed. "No, the alligator. They're prehistoric. They have jaws of steel and clamp down on their prey and do this death spiral thing. You don't want to get near them. You don't want to get near the edge of the swamp because you don't know they're there and then... chomp." I clapped in a big alligator-mouth gesture.

He took my hand and tugged me up the walk to the front door. "We must hurry then, or your grandfather will be hurt."

I'd rushed over for just such a reason, but I'd met Howard before. Gramps had a healthy respect for the animal, but he was too kindhearted and kept feeding him snacks, which meant the alligator returned. Like a pet.

Alligators were not pets.

I was all for Gramps getting himself out there and socializing, but not with Howard. I was sure there had to be a nice widow around who might like to take a different kind of bite out of my grandfather.

"Hello? We're here!" I called, but I knew Gramps was out back. I cut down the central hallway—taking a few seconds to appreciate the air-conditioning—and to the back door off the kitchen.

"Hi, Gramps," I called. "It's me."

Gramps turned in his lawn chair, then pushed to standing. Howard was at the back edge of the lawn, maybe fifteen steps from the porch, sunning himself. I guessed Howard was about six feet long. Not huge, but no baby either.

The property was in an older neighborhood where each home backed up to a greenway with a walking path. Beyond that and down a small hill was the edge of the swamp. There was a reasonably deep channel for small boats to cut through. There were manatees on rare occasions. Birds. It would be like backing up to a thick forest in the rest of the country. It was peaceful, except for an occasional visit by Howard.

"There's my girl," Gramps said, coming our way across

the concrete patio that surrounded his small pool. The water itself was beneath a screened-in dome, but he was outside it now since he couldn't toss beef jerky otherwise. I ran forward and hugged him—gently, as I knew the cancer treatments made his bones ache. He was too thin, his dark eyes sunken in his face. His normally caramel-brown skin was not able to completely hide the sickly yellow tinge just underneath.

When he released me, he wasn't looking at me but over my shoulder at Braun. I was looking at Howard, making sure he stayed far, far away.

"When you said you had someone with you, I didn't expect an alien." His voice was stern, but I knew he was poking fun. While Braun didn't *look* all that different from humans, he was just so much larger than almost any human. It was pretty obvious he wasn't from Earth by that alone. "He'll be better company than Howard."

And safer.

I kissed Gramps on the cheek, took his hand, and walked slowly forward to present Braun.

"Braun, this is my grandfather, Jassa Singh Kaur. Gramps, this is Braun, an Atlan warlord."

"It is an honor, sir." Braun bowed.

"Oh, I'm not formal around here. Stand up, boy," Gramps ordered.

Braun stood to his full height, and Gramps and I craned our necks back in what had to seem like a comedy from Braun's perspective.

"You look like one of those basketball players."

Braun grinned. "So Angela tells me."

"You play then?"

"No, sir. It is not something we have on Atlan. I do not know what basketball is."

"Have you seen an alligator before?" Thankfully Gramps wasn't going to explain the sport and easily switched topics.

"No, sir."

"Well, I don't know much about basketball, but that"—he pointed to Howard—"is an alligator. Did you bring the beef jerky?" He asked the last of me.

I laughed. "No. Mom will kill me if I enable you."

He humphed, then went and picked up the small packet he'd been using.

"Here." He held it out to Braun.

Braun eyed it, then stared at Gramps.

"Take a piece and feed Howard."

Braun's eyes widened as he stared at the beef jerky packet, then me, then Howard. He spoke to Gramps with his hands up in a stop gesture. "I fought the Hive with honor, but I am not feeding that thing."

I bit my lip to keep from laughing.

"Hello!"

Gramps shoved the beef jerky packet at me when he heard my mother's muffled voice coming from inside. "Hide that before she sees it." He'd always been my partner in crime with my parents, and that was what made him so special. I had no siblings, so he'd helped me get into enough mischief over the years.

Braun swiveled around, confused.

I rolled my eyes, grabbed the jerky packet, and stuffed it into the large planter next to the patio table. The flowers were blooming, and it looked like Gramps hadn't trimmed the thing in months. Lots of hiding space for the evidence.

"Good thinking." Gramps winked at me as my parents came outside in a rush, catching their breath. I imagined them speeding across town from the hardware store to get here. Gramps lived alone and since he was sick, we all worried, but he refused to move. My mother was probably questioning this now because of his developing relationship with Howard.

Mom took in the scene, but her gaze landed on Braun and stayed. Dad followed her out and stopped dead in his tracks as well. I understood their surprise. An alligator was one thing, but an alien? The looks on their faces were comical.

I reached behind me and grabbed Braun's hand, pulling him forward. My father was not a tall man, nothing near Braun's size, and my mom was barely taller than me. Braun bent at the waist in another bow.

Now that I didn't have to panic about Gramps being eaten, I took a second to appreciate Braun. Good God, he was gorgeous. And respectful to my parents. Something the asshole Kevin had never managed the two or three times I'd brought him home. In fact, my mother had pulled me aside and warned me I was making a mistake when I told her Kevin was living with me. I should have listened to her. No surprise there.

Having Braun beside me felt different. Introducing him felt... important. I wanted them to meet him, to know the man—ahem, alien—I found fascinating and then some. It was important Braun knew them as well. We were too close to keep something so big, literally and figuratively, from them.

"Mom, Dad, this is Braun. He is a warlord from the planet Atlan." I looked at my parents and thanked every-thing holy that I'd been born so lucky, remembering that not everyone had family. "Braun, this is my father, Hari Singh Kaur, and my mother, Michelle Marie Kaur."

"It is an honor to meet you both." Braun did not lift his gaze nor his head from the bow, and my parents looked at me with a question in their eyes. I shrugged. I had no idea what Atlan customs Braun followed, but I was enchanted. Besotted, even, by his effort. Even when there was an alligator not far away.

I didn't want to embarrass Braun by commenting on his behavior when he was being respectful. Perhaps my mother thought the same thing, because she stepped up to him and set her hand on his arm. He rose and while he loomed over her, gave her a small smile.

"My father-in-law has you to thank for preventing a solid scolding." She leaned around Braun to direct a pointed look at Gramps.

My father covered a cough with the back of his hand, but I suspected it wasn't a cough at all.

"I am curious to know, Daughter, how you found an alien," Dad said, then looked to Braun. "I want to know all about outer space." He wiggled his black eyebrows. "Especially the gadgets and gizmos."

Braun looked confused.

"The technology. My father is an engineer."

"Enough of this. Let's eat! I'm starving." Gramps grumbled at all of us, taking advantage of his age to boss the young people around. To me, it was good to hear that he was hungry after his treatments.

"That's because you probably fed all your snacks to Howard." My mother was trying hard not to encourage him, but we could all see her eyes crinkling at the corners.

I glanced over my shoulder to look at the animal. He

hadn't moved at all, and his eyes were now closed as he took a nap. Clearly an alien was of no interest to him.

Gramps went ahead of us into the kitchen. The beach was out, and there was no way I could leave with Braun now. We were stuck, although I didn't mind. I hoped Braun didn't. He'd been interested in me. Only me. Only me for sex... and a little fun in Miami. But parents? A sick grandfather? A pseudo-pet alligator named Howard?

Something else entirely.

"Come with me, young man," Mom said, taking Braun's burly arm. "If you are dating my daughter, I am going to ask you at least a thousand questions."

Were we dating? We hadn't gone anywhere but my apartment, and while we'd definitely gotten to know each other, it wasn't dinner and a movie either. Not that I was going to share that with Mom. There were *some* things I kept secret.

"Don't forget the gadgets!" my father called over his shoulder as he followed Gramps, and we all laughed.

My mother and Braun were next, and he had to duck through the doorway.

I was the last inside, closing the door behind me, my heart bursting at the seams with happiness for the first time in so long it was difficult to remember. I'd had no idea how important it was for my family to meet Braun. For Braun to like them.

My mother went to the fridge and grabbed some things for lunch as I pulled out a chair at the kitchen table for Gramps. No matter how tired he might be, he wasn't going to miss any discussion about space.

"Now, Braun, tell me everything about yourself," she

said, glancing over her shoulder as she put things on the counter.

I shook my head. "Mom, you can't do that. He will take you literally."

"Good." Her raised brows let me know she meant business. I glanced at Braun, who looked to me for guidance. I pointed to a chair, and he sat down, which eased all our necks.

"Go ahead," I told him. "They've never talked with an alien before."

"You, Daughter, can begin by telling us where you met."

"At work."

"Ah, you are the Atlan warlord for the television show," Mom said, snapping her fingers. Then she narrowed her eyes. "Staying at the hotel where my baby works?"

"Yes."

I pulled a chair and sat close to Gramps so I could hold his frail hand and hoped, now that the chemotherapy was done, he could gain some weight and feel better. I looked up from our entwined fingers to find Braun watching me with a heat in his eyes that I recognized, but the tenderness there was new. I'd mentioned that Gramps was sick, and I was sure Braun could tell.

"Go ahead. Tell us everything. I want to know, too."

And I did. I knew nothing about him other than the fact that he was an alien, he was very skilled in bed, and he'd fought in a war in outer space, been captured and tortured somehow and implanted with other alien stuff like those weird *Star Trek* Borg. And most of that I knew because I'd watched the promotions for the *Bachelor Beast* television show.

Although, as I now thought about it, I'd seen him naked multiple times and hadn't noticed any weird computer parts. So if he had them, where were they? He looked totally, gorgeously normal to me. And he was supposed to turn into some kind of beast? I hadn't seen that either, not with him. His voice had grown deeper and his face had seemed a bit wider once or twice —maybe—but that was it. So what was the big deal about this beast side of him? Was it like some kind of animal instinct?

I remembered watching as Warlord Wulf had turned into his beast when he'd torn across the set to get to his just-found mate, Olivia. Now *he'd* been a beast. But Braun had never been anything like that. He hadn't grown a foot or lost his ability to speak well. It could also be that because I wasn't his true mate, his beast hadn't come out for me.

I felt myself frown and shoved the thought aside. Now wasn't the time to think about that.

Braun cleared his throat, breaking me from my thoughts. I wanted to know everything about this man. No. Alien. He was an alien. And he wasn't mine. He had a hotel floor full of beautiful, polished, perfect women to choose from. A petite, curvy, half-black Punjabi girl working as a maid to pay rent on a shithole, one-bedroom apartment needed to remember that.

But damn, looking at him, it was hard not to want more.

8

SURROUNDED BY ANGELA'S FAMILY, inundated with questions, I should have been pleased.

Instead I felt as if I were drowning. I took a deep breath,
tried to hide my nerves along with the beast that wanted me
to run from this home. From these kind people who looked
at me with open curiosity. Not because of integrations or the
fact that I was the latest bachelor beast, but because I was
from someplace foreign to them.

They wanted to know about my culture, my way of life.
About me.

Perhaps that was why I was uncomfortable. I wasn't used
to being anything but an integrated warlord. Something to
be fearful of. An oddity.

So I shared what I thought they would find interesting. I
told them I was from Atlan, which they knew. I told them

that I fought for the Coalition, which they also knew from the television show.

As I spoke, Angela's mother, Michelle, placed food on the table while her father set out plates, silverware and glasses of water.

"How long were you a POW?" The elder, Jassa Kaur, was very clearly unwell. His body was too thin, even for a small human male. Angela had mentioned that she put money toward his medicine. I didn't know how ill he was because a ReGen wand or a pod would solve whatever the elderly man had before he became this sickly. But his gaze was focused and intelligent, and he listened to everything I said with a level of interest I had never experienced before.

The fact that he had befriended a dangerous animal showed his character.

Humans were an oddly passionate people. War and death were accepted and even expected on my home planet. A male without a mate to tame his beast was ultimately executed when the fever overtook him. We learned young not to question these facts, nor place too much weight on any relationship except that with our mate.

"Well? How long?"

"Gramps, please. Leave him alone. This can't be an easy topic for him. Remember, we are the aliens to him. We are the odd ones." Angela leaned forward and looked up at me with sadness in her gaze. Or was that pity? I wanted neither from her.

"What is this P.O.W.?"

"Prisoner of war," Angela clarified.

I nodded. "Ah, yes. Being a prisoner, I lost track of the days. Too many."

Gramps nodded as if he understood. "How did you

escape?"

"A Coalition ReCon Unit found me and brought me in."

"Hospital?"

"Medical?" I asked, hoping my understanding of the language was sound. "Yes. For three days."

The old man leaned forward with interest now. "Three days? That's it?"

"The integrations that could be removed were extracted from my body, and I was placed in a ReGen pod to heal. I was unconscious for nearly two days. When I emerged from the pod, I was transported to The Colony."

Michelle sat in the empty chair beside me and called to her mate. "Hari, he's talking about gadgets and gizmos. Stop fussing with the ice maker and get over here." Angela's father had been busy in the food cooling machine called a refrigerator. Besides the quick food Angela had made us when I stayed with her, I had not seen a meal prepared by hand since I was a boy, before I entered training. The barracks used S-Gen machines to provide food for so many hungry warlords. But the items on the table were slices of what I guessed were meat and cheese, bowls of mixed items I didn't recognize, and bottles of some kind. I had no idea what they were used for, but I assumed they contained food.

Hari hurried over and joined us. Michelle reached for him at once, her hand rubbing his shoulder in a gentle touch that he accepted as his due. I closed my eyes so Angela would not see the longing on my face for a touch such as this. I had been born for war, trained from a young age, hardened and taught to kill to protect my people. I regretted none of it. But now, with Angela so near, my beast needed her, needed to be accepted and soothed by our mate. To know the same touch from another to me.

The elder cleared his throat as he used a spoon to put some of the unidentified food on his plate. "You said the integrations that *could be removed*. You still have some of them?"

"Yes." The reminder of my contamination and failure as a warrior erased all longing from my body, replacing it with anger. "I am considered contaminated by my people. The Coalition worlds do not want warriors with Hive integrations on their planets. We are considered too dangerous. So we live out our days on The Colony, mining and working for the rest of the Coalition Fleet."

"Sounds like prison camp to me," the old man said and used his metal drinking cup to bang on his pants where they covered his lower leg. I glanced around the table to see what he was doing. To my surprise, a metallic banging sound was the result.

"Titanium," the older man explained. "Lost the leg in battle a long time ago. Can you beat that?" He was chuckling, which confused me and my beast. How was the loss of a limb amusing?

At my silence all four of the humans looked up expectantly. Angela went to the cabinet and returned with an odd-shaped package, like a sealed bag. She tugged at the top, and it opened easily. Reaching in, she pulled out yellow flat disks that were misshapen. When she put one in her mouth, it crunched. When she saw me eyeing the item, she took one from her plate and held it out to me.

I put it in my mouth, and it did, indeed, crunch loudly. The flavor was salty and greasy. "What is this?" I asked after swallowing.

"Potato chip," Angela explained. She reached across the table and poured a few onto my plate.

Her grandfather cleared his throat, and I remembered his question. "Ah, you're wondering what my war injuries are."

The older man nodded; the others just waited patiently. Hari was eating a piece of the sliced meat, and Michelle was squirting something from one of the bottles onto her plate. It was bright yellow in color. I was curious about their food, and they were curious about me. I had a feeling I could tell them I did not wish to share, but they weren't making me out to be an oddity. No, they were intelligent humans who wanted to know about me. About what I'd been through.

I realized that although I had fucked Angela more than once, I had been very careful not to show her my integrations. I'd been a coward, scared perhaps she would be afraid of them. Of me. Would find me distasteful or repulsive.

I'd been wrong.

Her grandfather leaned down and pulled at his pants leg, bunching the fabric in his hands to reveal the metal rod that had replaced the lower piece of his leg. "This is what the war gave me. And I was angry for a long time."

"How did you defeat your rage?" Even as I asked the question, the beast within paced. He was angry all the time. Every moment of every day since I'd been born, he'd been fighting me. And his rage grew stronger with each passing hour. The reminder of what the Hive had done to me made my blood burn like acid as he fought to break free. It was a different sensation than my beast. The Hive had stolen something from me, and I would never get it back. I knew my voice had changed, but I needed an answer. "How did you forget your failure?"

"Failure?" He tapped his metallic leg again, the ringing of metal on metal loud in the sudden silence around us.

"This is not failure, Son. I survived. Just like you did. I'm proud of you." He leaned back and raised his glass to me in a very human salute I'd seen the females on The Colony perform. "And you can't defeat the rage. You can't suppress it. You can't fight it. You have to accept it and call it friend. That fire is what kept you fighting, it kept you alive and it brought you here. My fire brought me home, back to my family. How is that a failure? It's a bloody miracle, is what it is. A bloody miracle."

Angela had scooped some of the mystery food onto my plate, but she put the spoon back in the bowl. "Pasta salad," she said.

"Thank you," I replied but paid the food no attention. I didn't stop to think about my decision, nor did I consider the repercussions. I *needed* to show myself to my mate. To have her know all of me. What I'd become.

Lifting the shirt Angela had given me to wear, I pulled the fabric off over my head and placed the bunched-up shirt in my lap. Bare from the waist up, I turned around and presented my mate with my back... and the strange silver streaks that spread from my spinal column to disappear in the muscles that run up and down my back.

"Oh my God." Angela's voice was whisper soft, and I closed my eyes, not wanting to allow the heated tears I felt gathering to fall. I would not show such weakness. Not here, in front of her family.

Not ever.

The beast bellowed inside my mind, demanding to be set free, to release his fury. I clenched my fists and ignored him and the pain slicing through my skull, as I had for years. I did not lose control. Not for a moment. Not ever.

Not now, in front of these humans who were... special.

My beast was too strong. If I let him go, I might never regain control.

"That is fascinating." Angela's mother spoke with a clinical tone I'd come to recognize among medical personnel. "Can I? I don't want to be rude, but do you mind?"

I glanced over my shoulder at Angela, not understanding the question. She looked up at me, and there were tears in her eyes. "She wants to touch them."

I nodded my acceptance and turned back to stare at the water in the swimming pool. I had spent time in one recently, with Dr. Surnen's mate, Mikki. I knew how to swim, but now was not the time for play.

A warm hand pressed to my spine and traced the ridges of both my bones and the Hive integrations that rose from my flesh. "What do they do?"

I answered clinically, the same way Dr. Surnen had told me what could—and could not—be removed from my body without killing me. "They are augmented feedback loops. The striations expand deep into the muscle fibers. I also have them throughout my buttocks, hips and thighs. They make my response time faster. My muscles are also augmented to take additional load."

"So you are stronger and faster than you would be without them?" she asked.

"Yes. By a factor of three to four times."

"That is some gadget." Angela's father whistled.

Everyone's food was forgotten.

"And your eyes?" Angela asked the question, her voice soft as if afraid I would take offense. It was the only bit of integration that she'd seen.

"The silver ring is the result of an augmented visual system."

"That means you would have had integrations directly in the optical centers of your brain." Angela's mother was making a statement, not asking a question.

I nodded. "Yes. As you can see, once the external integrations were taken out, the others could not be removed or altered without ending my life." I spoke clearly, like a teacher lecturing students. "With spinal and brain implants, I was deemed a threat and sent to The Colony."

"And this happens to all of you?" Angela's hand traced the line of one silver streak on my back, and I held very still.

"No. Most of us die when the integrations are removed. I was lucky. Dr. Surnen is very skilled with Hive technology."

"And this Hive, that's who we're fighting in outer space?" Angela's father asked.

"Yes. For centuries." I sighed and put my shirt back on before turning around. I met her grandfather's gaze. "It has been a very long war."

Angela's grandfather stood and looked down at me. "You promise me you'll look after our little girl?"

My mouth fell open. He'd surprised me. I'd expected the opposite of what he was giving, which was his approval.

I dipped my head. "I will protect her with my life."

"Gramps!" Angela exclaimed, but I kept my eyes on her grandfather.

"Good. It has been an honor, soldier." He raised a hand to his forehead in what I recognized as a human military salute. He lowered his hand and looked at his son. "I am tired, Hari. Help your father to his room, would you?"

"Of course." Angela's father rose quickly and moved to help his elderly father out of the room. They disappeared and I was left facing two females, my mate and her mother.

They both stood as well, and Angela's mother stepped

forward, wrapped her arms around my shoulders and squeezed. With me sitting and her standing, our heights aligned better. "I'm hugging you; deal with it."

Not wanting to remain seated while an elder female stood, I rose to my feet, and she released her hold because I'd become too tall. Angela laughed and I found my arms moving to embrace the small female who had brought my mate into the universe. I owed her a great debt.

She let go and was wiping tears from her cheeks. "I approve of this one." The elder female winked an eye at me and disappeared down the hall.

The moment we were alone, Angela came around the table to me and jumped, throwing herself into my arms. I stepped back away from my chair. "I can't believe all that. What you've been through, Braun. I just can't."

"Don't think about it." I did not want her to be unhappy or distressed by anything in life, but especially me.

She lifted her head from my shoulder and looked up into my face. I held her off the ground easily. She was so small I could have carried ten times the weight without effort. So small. Fragile. Female. So soft.

So powerful.

The beast settled the moment she was in my arms. Should anyone threaten her, hurt her... the resulting destruction would be catastrophic.

"I have to go to class soon," she said. "Time to take you home."

I kissed her, mindful of the window where I saw her mother watching us. Even with the audience, I could not resist tasting her. I was proud of myself for leaving my hands chastely clasped to her thighs. "The hotel is not my home, but there is something I must acquire there."

She leaned her forehead against mine, and I did not want to move. Ever.

"Okay. I can't miss school. I have to go. But I want you to come to my apartment after. Yes?"

She asked as if she doubted I'd join her. Nothing would stop me. "Of course. I will be there before nine, human time."

That made her giggle, and I set her down, watched her ass sway as she moved back toward the chairs and her buzzing communication device.

She picked the device up, touched it with her fingers, and frowned, clearly upset.

"What troubles you, mate?" I would crush whatever it was like a worm.

"Oh, nothing. That jerk, Kevin, is still trying to steal my TV."

"Should I scare him with my beast? I would be happy to do so."

That did make her laugh, a full, happy laugh that made me forget there was a human male in need of crushing.

"No. It's fine." She went back around the table and sat, tucking back into her lunch. "He's an asshole. He says he bought the TV so he should get to keep it. It's ridiculous. His dad's a state politician. Rich. I'm sure there are ten TVs in his huge waterfront mansion. I have to assume his dad cut him off or Kevin's just being even more of a dick than usual. Why come after my stupid-ass TV?" She ate a bite of food.

I mimicked her actions and tried a bite of the pasta salad. Unusual but good. "I do understand these Earth dynamics. Is it not true? Should the device belong to him if he purchased it?"

"Oh, he bought it, all right. He went into the store and

picked it out. Brought it back to the apartment." She slid the device into a pocket. "But he used *my* debit card to pay for it."

"I still do not understand." The human system of banking made no sense and seemed designed to enslave the population rather than help them acquire comfort or stability. Their system was one of the reasons Earth had not been offered full membership in the Interstellar Coalition of Planets. That and many other barbaric practices, such as fighting over resources, starving their citizens, denying them medical treatment. Slavery. The list was long, but the Coalition was timeless. They could wait for Earth to mature... or destroy itself.

Angela smiled. "It doesn't matter. Like Gramps said, I'm starving. Shall I tell you about what you're eating?"

"Would Howard like it?" I asked.

She laughed. "I think Howard eats anything."

She took time in explaining each of the dishes. Of the bottles of something called condiments. I liked the mustard, but the pickles were too sour for me.

After saying goodbye to her parents, she drove me back to the hotel, and I reluctantly left her so that she could attend her educational class. I would not waste my time while she was elsewhere. I had things to do to make her mine. First, I would secure my mating cuffs. They were Angela's, and I would see them on her wrists. Second, I would comm The Colony and tell Governor Maxim that he would need to send another contestant to this human television show. After meeting her family today, it was more clear than ever. I was no longer available.

Angela was my mate. Mine.

The beast agreed.

9

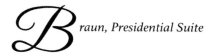

raun, Presidential Suite

"Why do you keep looking away?" Governor Maxim asked. "Am I boring you?"

I was back in my room, angry and anxious. I lacked patience. Angry that I had to spend a minute apart from my mate. My beast was pacing, waiting the minutes until we could return to her. After the time we'd spent together, after meeting her family, I was more sure of my decision than ever. Not that I questioned my beast, but Angela was... perfect.

She'd told me of her schooling, the years she'd taken to become a nurse. I made the mental comparison to the highly qualified and skilled medical technicians throughout the Coalition. It was an honorable profession, and I respected her desire to help others. She would be well received and kept busy on The Colony. I had no doubt

Dr. Surnen would find her an excellent addition to his staff.

Her parents were calm and kind. Her grandfather was honorable and wise, despite the loss of his mate and his battle with human cancer, a horrible enemy for a lonely elder to face alone. But Angela's grandfather fought to live, to love, to survive. He fought with courage.

Unlike my own father. He had been one of the most respected warlords ever to return to Altan to take a bride after serving the Coalition Fleet. He'd claimed her. Loved her. Lost her too soon.

The memories crashed in on me, but for the first time since I was a boy, they did not cause hurt. I finally understood what had driven my father to abandon me, his only son, when I was just a child, to send me away to a training academy without saying goodbye. To walk willingly into the Atlan prison cell and unleash his beast because his mate was dead.

My father had been executed on my second day of training. The commander of my training unit on Atlan had pulled me aside and told me of my father's chosen fate. To mourn him as well as my mother.

He'd *chosen* to die. Because of that, I'd hated my father for many years, feared that my own beast would rage and consume me just like his had done to him. With my mother's untimely death in a shuttle accident, I had lost both parents, my home and my entire life in the span of a few days. That was the start of my inner rage, of my beast clawing to get out with all the sadness and anger. Frustration and anger.

Since the day of my father's execution, I had kept my beast caged, unleashed only in battle, and sparingly, lest the wildness that burned in my blood overcome me and force me to make the same choice my father had. Execution. Death.

Peace.

Only now did I finally understand. Angela was everything and the only person in the universe that my beast would now obey. Without her, the beast would rage, as my father's had. Without Angela by my side, I would choose to share my father's fate without hesitation.

Without Angela, I was lost. I was alive but dead inside.

"Braun? Speak to me. What is happening? Are you unwell?" The irritation in the governor's voice had changed to concern, and I realized I'd been staring, unseeing, at the clock the humans kept next to their bed.

"I am looking at the time. There is a human clock next to me," I explained.

"You requested this conversation, and now you do not speak?"

I sighed, trying to be patient not only with being away from Angela, but with my governor. My life had changed the second I saw my mate when she'd come into my bedroom. I'd been blind to everything but her. I'd been too busy focusing on being with her, touching her, satisfying her—and my beast—that I had not dealt with the logistics of making her mine. The fact that there was anything in my way made me even more riled.

"I've found her." There. That explained it all. The comm call could be over now.

"Found who?" he asked.

"I found my mate."

Even through the small tablet I'd brought with me from The Colony, I couldn't miss the way his eyes widened.

"How? I thought the program hadn't begun. I was told there was a delay of some kind."

I nodded. "That is correct. My mate is not one of the contestants. She is employed by the hotel."

He paused, processed. "Fuck," he said, exhaling heavily. "You didn't destroy the set like Wulf, did you?"

I frowned. "No."

"You didn't claim her on camera?"

"No. She came to clean my room, and my beast recognized her as mine."

I remembered Angela's words about wanting to keep her pleasure private. Now that I'd spent additional time with her, I agreed. I wished to let everyone know she was mine, but not through her screams of satisfaction. The mating cuffs would do. That was also on my list of things to resolve.

I also remembered how upset Governor Maxim had been dealing with the humans and their bizarre paper contracts. They had made unreasonable demands on Wulf and his new mate. Wulf had complied because Olivia had not wanted to upset or anger the humans who operated the mating show. And also because he knew there were other males on The Colony who very much needed to find a mate.

Males like me.

Still, things had become crazed because Wulf's beast had taken over and made a mess of things. The set, the program's schedule. Everything. I kept my beast under strict control so that anything like what Wulf did wouldn't happen with me. But if Maxim denied my mate, I wouldn't be able to refrain from doing whatever was necessary to keep Angela. I hadn't even been on the main set yet, so at least that would be safe.

He glanced off-screen, spoke low to someone, then turned back. "I've called for Lindsey to join this comm."

She'd been the PR person who'd organized the program to grow interest in females volunteering to be brides. From what she'd said, there had been an uptick in bride tests, but the show hadn't gone as planned. Wulf had found his mate, Olivia, but she'd been a makeup artist for the program instead of a contestant. Now I'd found a hotel maid to be my mate. Again, not a contestant.

"I'm offering you the courtesy of a comm to share with you my intentions. I have returned to the hotel to obtain my cuffs so that I may properly claim Angela Kaur."

Maxim nodded, then looked away.

"What's up?" Lindsey said as she moved into view of the comms and dropped into a chair beside the governor. "Hey, Braun! Did you find that authentic Earth ice cream store Jorik told you about? The one where Gabriela worked?"

"He found something else. His mate," Maxim told her.

She raised her arms over her head. "Hallelujah! I never liked executions."

I was pleased with her enthusiasm, but it was a little more exuberant than I was expecting. And the grim reminder of my alternative wasn't as funny as she was trying to be. Humans had a way of speaking called sarcasm that wasn't used on Atlan. What she considered humorous came across differently through an NPU. I was thankful I understood English well enough to recognize she wasn't being literal.

Making light of an Atlan's mating fever and imminent execution was not a normal topic for jests. Still, Lindsey's heart was in her eyes, and she leaned toward the comm screen with obvious excitement.

"That's so awesome, Braun. You deserve it. Is she the pretty redhead contestant from Arizona? I saw her and thought you two might hit it off."

I frowned, filtering through all the contestants I'd run into in the hallway, and couldn't picture her. Of course, I couldn't imagine any female but Angela now.

"No. She's a maid who works for the hotel."

She blinked. "A maid. As in, that's her job?"

"As in a hotel maid who is not part of the *Bachelor Beast* program," Maxim clarified.

"Oh shit," she whispered. "I'll patch the producer in. Wait, he's taking a day off because of the delay. I'll have to let Chet know."

"I heard the program was stalled. What was the problem?" Maxim asked. "Not your mate?"

"Pink eye," I said.

He frowned. Obviously he hadn't been apprised of the details about what was happening on Earth, but he was the governor, not the one organizing the program. I'd called him, not to tell him about the show but to inform him that I had found my mate because it had been his decision to send me. I felt obligated to tell him first. I owed him my life.

And now he would choose another to take my place. Perhaps Lindsey's red-haired contestant from this Arizona would interest another. I had found my female, with her black hair, dark eyes, and soft brown skin. I wanted no other. She was kind and compassionate, accepted my contamination, and I hoped was coming to care for me. She was perfect.

"Hang on," Lindsey said. She fiddled with something and didn't pay Maxim's confusion any notice. I waited patiently. Barely.

Chet's face filled a box on the tablet screen I was using.

"What the fuck happened to you?" Maxim asked him, leaning in to get a better look.

Chet's eye *was* pink and crusty and... I tried not to wince.

"It's nothing. An infection. I'll be fine in a day or two," Chet said.

Maxim looked to Lindsey for clarification. She leaned in and whispered in his ear. He turned back to the comms and cleared his throat, clearly not wanting to mention it further. "Warlord Braun has found his mate," he announced.

One of Chet's eyes got big—the non-pink one. "The show hasn't started."

"I found her outside the female contestants," I explained.

"Where?"

Angela had said she could be fired for spending time with a guest. While she would be heading to The Colony with me instead of working at the hotel, I didn't want her to be in trouble. I would not have anyone devaluing or bothering her in any way.

"Her name is Angela Kaur. How I met her is irrelevant," I told him instead. "I am collecting my cuffs and will make the claim official this evening." I had never liked the idea of my family mating cuffs being away from me. I had agreed because I'd seen the fancy box they'd been placed in when Wulf appeared on the show. I remembered how Wulf's had been shown to humans during the program, and mine were to be displayed identically.

However, I had not yet surrendered them. Thank the gods. I would not have to deal with Chet or any other humans. I would take the cuffs to Angela, ask her to be mine forever, and place them on her wrists. Tonight. I would do so tonight. The thought made me smile even as Chet groaned.

Chet's face mottled the same color as his infected eye. "We have no show. Again!"

"Now, Chet, there is an endless supply of worthy males here on The Colony," Lindsey said, her tone pacifying. "We will replace Braun with someone else. We have time to make a switch. There was a delay, remember?"

She stared at him pointedly. The program was on hold because he wasn't hygienic.

"Who the hell are you going to send at such a short notice?" he practically shouted.

"People aren't going to want to watch this show if the beasts keep... being beasts. And the contestants... women aren't going to volunteer to participate if they don't even have a chance."

Lindsey narrowed her eyes. "There was no guarantee that any of the warlords would meet their mate among the contestants. I will remind you the ratings of the first round with Warlord Wulf were the best of any program in US television history, and all because the mate wasn't a contestant. It was considered romantic. Fate."

I'd known Lindsey for a while, and for a small human, I didn't want to be the one at the end of her tongue lashing. While she and Angela looked nothing alike, their spunk and attitude were similar.

"What do I tell the contestants? The viewing audience?" Chet countered.

"The truth. That Warlord Braun has found his true mate and has returned to The Colony."

"Then who will take his place? The show will start as

soon as this"—he pointed to his eye—"is cleared up. A day. Maybe two at the latest."

Maxim looked to Lindsey. "Warlord Bahre would be an excellent option."

Lindsey's face lit up. "Yes! Perfect." She focused on Chet. "There is an excellent replacement just waiting to meet twenty-four women. We will send another warlord to be the next bachelor beast. Just like Braun, I promise you he'll be big, handsome, a warlord, and a very available bachelor."

I sighed, glad for Lindsey's pushiness and order. If I'd had my way, I'd have gone to Chet's room and pounded him until he accepted my withdrawal from the show, but then I'd perhaps get the horrid pink eye. My mate had informed me that the condition was highly contagious.

"With all of this resolved, I will collect my cuffs and collect my mate. Thank you for your assistance, Governor. Lindsey. Please wish whomever you send to Earth good hunting," I said, then ended the comm. The details of Bahre's, or any other warlord's, trip to Earth to take my place were not my problem. I had one thing to take care of, one thing that mattered to me, and she wasn't here.

Looking at the clock once more, I saw it was almost time to return to Angela's quarters. Her schooling would be complete. I would ensure she was fed and comfortable, then well pleasured before I put my cuffs on her wrists.

With my plan in place, I went to grab the cuffs. should wait and ask Angela to place mine around my wrists, but my beast was already fighting me with a newly enraged fury. He wanted out. He wanted Angela, hot, wet, naked, and submissive as he claimed her. I couldn't afford to wait. I needed the control now.

With a smile I felt all the way to my toes, I snapped the

heavy cuffs around my wrists and welcomed the pain. They were designed to cause enough pain to get the beast's attention, to remind me that I had a mate even when I could not see her. They were a physical and mental link to the female who owned me, heart and beast and soul. And it was time to make Angela mine forever.

Placing her much smaller pair of matching mating cuffs in my pocket, I stalked out of my room with an actual smile on my face.

This trip to Earth couldn't have gone any better.

a ngela, Her Apartment

I COULD HAVE KISSED my professor for letting us out of class early. I'd barely heard a word of what she'd said, and my notes looked like something I might have done in seventh grade, with my name and Braun's doodled inside of hearts all over the page. I'd barely said goodbye to my classmates before practically running to my car. I ached in all the good places after being with Braun. Again and again. To say he was voracious was an understatement.

But only for *me.* That was the one thing I was having a hard time wrapping my mind around. Was he serious? Was I his chosen mate? *The One?* Really? And what would that mean exactly? Would he expect me to leave my family and go live on another planet?

Would I? Could I do that and be happy?

So many questions. Possibilities chased themselves

around inside my head like a puppy going after its tail. Yes. No. Maybe. I didn't know. That was the big one. I didn't know anything. Not for sure.

Well, that was a lie. I knew I was falling in love with an alien. I knew he touched me like I mattered, like I was his world and he'd never get enough. I knew he listened to everything I said and remembered what I told him. I knew he acted respectfully to my parents and Gramps, which was something stupid Kevin had never quite managed.

And the orgasms? Holy shit, the orgasms. So many. So good. I'd never felt like a sexual goddess, not once in my life. But I did now. I felt sexy and beautiful and powerful. And all because a giant alien man had chosen me. Me!

Crazy. It was all just too crazy to be real. Too good to be true. Braun was wonderful. Amazing.

As I turned the corner and went down my street, I couldn't help but smile. Braun was a beast. In bed and out.

With him, I'd been wild. I'd never been a prude, but I hadn't initiated sex much either. The sex I'd had hadn't been all that great. I hadn't known before, but now I sure as hell did. Braun was a skilled lover. Generous. Attentive. I came first and more than once. He saw to it.

He took care of me in everything he did. For such a huge guy, he was so gentle with me. I was turning into a lovesick fool. And sex crazed.

But just like when I was thirteen, I was probably thinking fairy tales. Braun was to be on the *Bachelor Beast* program. While he'd spent the past two days with me, he had twenty-four women who wanted his attention, too.

I pulled into my brightly lit lot and slowed, frowning. I tipped my chin to look out the passenger window. My couch was sticking out of the back of a pickup truck. What the—

Fuck me.

I recognized that fancy truck. Kevin's. The one with the lift, the off-road wheels that never saw dirt. He had a vehicle worth more than I made in a year and had decided to steal my secondhand couch? What the fuck was going on with him?

Just then he came down the building's central stairwell with my Crock-Pot and set it in the back with the sofa and whatever else he'd stolen. As usual, he wore a golf shirt and Bermuda shorts with loafers and no socks. He dressed as if he'd come from the country club but was stealing my dang Crock-Pot. As I got closer, I noticed the little lobsters embroidered on his tan shorts.

Nice.

His hair had more product in it than I ever used. It was slicked back, which only showed his receding hairline. His usual sly grin was missing, and I recognized that beady-eyed look. The look that said he knew he was doing something wrong, but he had somehow justified everything to himself and convinced his pea-sized brain—and elephant-sized ego —that he had been wronged. That nothing was his fault. That the world owed him something. Or, based on the amount of my stuff I saw in the back of that truck, that I owed him everything I owned.

Asshole. I'd been so right to dump his ass. Now I just wanted him to go away. To *stay* away. Compared to Braun, he was a joke. An absolute sham of a man.

I pulled into the closest parking spot and got out, leaving my computer bag on the floor and locking the car behind me. I didn't want him stealing my laptop. If he was going for a fucking slow cooker, he'd definitely want my computer.

After locking the door, I ran over to him. "What the fuck are you doing?"

He turned his head to glare at me, then went back up the stairs. "I thought you had class tonight."

I stormed after him, up three flights of stairs and into my apartment, slamming the door shut behind me. He reached behind the TV to disconnect the wires. "That's not yours. Neither is the couch you've stolen... miraculously, on your own." He'd refused to help me move into the apartment, claiming his bad knee just couldn't take all those stairs.

After being with Braun for two days, Kevin looked scrawny. Small. Weak. While it wasn't huge, in order for him to get that sofa down three flights of stairs, he had to be on something. Maybe he had a friend who'd helped him with the couch and then left.

"It's mine now."

"The fucking Crock-Pot? You don't even know how to cook! Are you taking it for your maid?"

"I couldn't pay the maid. She's gone."

Just as I thought. He owed his bookie.

I stood between him and the door, my breath coming hard. I wasn't fit for sprinting up three flights of stairs. In the heat and humidity, even at nine at night, sweat trickled between my breasts. There was no way he was going to carry my couch back up the stairs, and I wasn't sure how I could personally stop him. He might be smaller than Braun, but he was bigger than me. He'd never been violent before, but I wasn't willing to take the risk.

I pulled my cell from my pocket and called the police. I didn't know what he was on, but surely he was on something. No one was this insane. The police answered, and I ignored Kevin to talk to the operator. "My ex-roommate broke into my apartment and is stealing my things." I wasn't going to say he was my ex-boyfriend. That only added salt to the wound that I'd voluntarily let him into my life.

I gave my address, and I had to hope they got here before the place was stripped bare.

He looked up from his task and narrowed his eyes. "They're not going to believe shit you say. I'm a Barrister. Nothing's going to stick."

With his daddy's name, he was right. Colin Barrister was well-known in politics. In social circles with a few extra zeroes on their paychecks. They made things happen in south Florida. I had to wonder what the hell happened with Kevin.

"This is my stuff," he continued. "You owe me."

"I don't owe you anything, you jerk. You disappeared with my rent. And you stole the money for my grandfather's meds. You know he has cancer. What kind of person does that?"

Kevin had taken hundreds of dollars from the coffee can I kept in the freezer. He knew I'd saved it for Gramps, but he'd taken every dime and lost it gambling. The moment I'd found the cash gone, that had been the end of our relationship. Game over. I'd suspected he'd been taking cash from my wallet but hadn't been able to prove it. When I'd confronted him one time, he'd said I was just forgetful and bad with my money. The asshole.

I had no doubt he'd blown through whatever cash he had of his own that Daddy'd given him and was in deep with someone, which was probably why he was back. There were casinos around Miami, but I had no doubt all kinds of illegal games were out there as well.

"We lived together," he snapped. "What's yours is mine and all that."

"This is Florida. It's not a community property state. What's mine is *mine*. Leave the TV alone," I shouted, waving my arms in the air.

"No."

God, it seemed I had more chance of talking to the wall than him. "How did you even get in here?"

Now he grinned. "Key."

I closed my eyes for a second. Of course. He'd given me his key back when I'd tossed him out, but it had been either a random key he'd given me or he'd gotten a copy made. I wasn't going to think about the fact that he'd had a key to my place for months.

With the couch gone, the place looked bigger.

"Get out, Kevin," I said, hoping maybe—*maybe*—he'd just go.

He crossed his arms over his chest. "No. I need this shit, and you're giving it to me. You *owe* me."

Kevin had said that twice now. I tossed my hands in the air. "For what? For you being an asshole? For you stealing money from me?"

"You tossed my shit outside and it rained. Everything was ruined."

"You stole medicine money I'd saved for an old man who has cancer!"

He didn't even blink at how much of an asshole move that was and went back to disconnecting my TV. He yanked the plug from the wall and hoisted the TV into his arms.

"Get out of my way." He took a step toward me, but I refused to retreat.

"No. It's not yours. The police are coming," I said again,

not sure if he'd even heard me calling 9-1-1. "I don't know who you owe money to, but that TV isn't worth much. Leave, Kevin."

"Get out of my way, bitch."

Someone knocked. Relief coursed through me at how fast the police had responded. But when I opened the door, it wasn't law enforcement but Braun. Even better. He could just look at Kevin and scare the hell out of him.

"Hello, Angela." His voice was gentle and calm, but he looked as serious as usual. "I have something I need to tell you."

"Who the fuck is that?" Kevin snarled. "Another man, Ang? Who'd want a dried-up slut like you?"

Braun's eyes narrowed and his jaw clenched. So much so I thought his teeth would crack. A deep rumble came from his chest as he gently moved me out of the way so he could enter, ducking his head.

I was so glad he was here that I almost burst into tears. He was on my side. Mine. And he was big. And brawny. And he was wearing something I'd only ever seen on television, a pair of big, heavy mating cuffs.

Was that what he wanted to talk to me about?

Why was he wearing them? I thought the beasts—Atlans—only put those on after they had claimed a mate. And since he hadn't claimed me, what was happening?

"Great, you bitch. Already moved on, have you? I knew you were a whore."

I cringed, the whore comment stinging despite the fact that Kevin was full of shit and had no right to call me anything, least of all a *slut* or a *whore*. Rude. Braun snarled and I had to move toward the kitchen to see Kevin around

Braun's body. Kevin's eyes were as wide as saucers, and his mouth hung open.

"Did you just call this female a derogatory term? Twice?" Braun's voice was deep. And angry.

Kevin swallowed hard but said nothing.

"Please introduce me, Angela." While he spoke to me, his gaze was on Kevin.

"This is Kevin."

"The one you told me about?"

"Yes."

"The one who stole your money, money meant for a respected and unhealthy elder?"

"Yes."

"Am I correct in assuming that your couch is the one in the back of a vehicle in the parking lot?"

"Yes."

Braun's voice became deeper and deeper with every word.

Oscar perched on the edge of a chair and watched Kevin.

"Stupid fucking cat." He kicked out and knocked the chair over. Oscar gave an angry hiss but streaked off unharmed.

Braun swept his arm out and used it to move me even more out of the way, placing his body firmly between me and Kevin. I shifted closer to the kitchen.

Kevin still held the TV, now holding it out in front of his body like a shield.

"Who the fuck are you?" Kevin asked, full of false bravado. Any other human guy would have shit his pants by now, only indicating even more clearly that he had to be on some kind of drugs. Or maybe he was just so desperate he was willing to risk getting his ass kicked over the small amount of cash he'd get for my stuff at a pawnshop.

"I am Warlord Braun, and you will put that television down. You will also return the items you have stolen."

"This shit is mine. She owes me."

Braun crossed his arms, and a deep rumbling sound came from his chest. I could have sworn he was growing bigger, but that would have been impossible.

No...

Oh shit.

That would be his beast.

Arms loose at his sides, he took one threatening step toward Kevin. Kevin squeaked and retreated but did not put the television down. Instead he backed toward the still-open door, holding the television. "Look, man, I don't want any trouble. I'm taking what's mine and I'm leaving."

"No." Braun followed Kevin out the door, and I hurried behind him, watching Kevin back toward the open concrete staircase as a police car with sirens blaring and lights flashing pulled into the parking lot directly below us. The walkway was open, as was the staircase, and I saw two officers get out of the car and hurry toward the bottom of the stairs.

Kevin heard them too, twisting his neck around and daring to look away from Braun for just long enough to peek down into the parking lot. Probably to gauge how much time he had left to get away with stealing my stuff. The police had parked on the wrong side of the building, but still, Kevin would have them to deal with in less than a minute.

"Kevin, just leave the television," I said. "We'll even help you unload the truck. But the police are here, and you're not taking everything I own to pay off another stupid gambling debt."

His eyes grew round as Braun watched him, but he took another step backward, toward the stairs. "This is mine."

"Don't be an idiot. Just put it down and walk away." I leaned around Braun's wide back to talk to Kevin and couldn't believe I'd ever seen anything other than the fear driving him. When I first met him, he'd been charming, well dressed, and a practiced flirt. Add that to his family money and he'd been almost irresistible to me at the time. Until I'd found out the truth, that he was empty and desperate and afraid. Everything else was a facade. "Call your father. He can help you. However much it is, or whoever you owe, he can help."

Kevin was shaking his head. "No. He already said no."

I nearly gasped with shock. Kevin was one of the most entitled people I'd ever met. One phone call got him anything he wanted. Kevin didn't face consequences. Ever.

I heard a noise and turned to see the police officers coming up the stairwell.

"Fuck." Kevin must have heard them too. He turned and tried to make a run for it.

But he was high or drunk or just frantic. He missed the first step and tumbled with a scream. The television slammed into his body with a thump that made me cringe as Kevin flailed on his way down the stairs.

The last thing I heard was a sickening crack before he ended up in a heap on the landing between floors.

With the TV on his chest, he stared up, wide-eyed. Unmoving. Blood quickly began to pool on the concrete beneath his head, and his body was contorted into an unnatural angle.

"Oh my God." I was shaking as Braun exhaled and pulled me against his chest, blocking my view. "We have to check him."

"He's dead. He will not bother you again."

That wasn't what I wanted. Well, it *was*—the not bothering me part. Not the *dead* part.

I had completely forgotten about the police until a woman cleared her throat. "Ms. Kaur?"

I nodded to the woman. "Yes. I called nine-one-one."

"Ma'am, no matter what happened here, I have to inform you of your rights. You have the right to remain silent. Anything you say may be used against you in a court of law. You have the right to an attorney."

The female officer continued to tell me my rights as I turned from Braun's embrace to see her partner—who hadn't come past Kevin's body on the stairs—leaning down to check his pulse. The officer then tilted Kevin's head to the side to see the dent at the base of his skull. Blood coated his palms. This was bad. Really bad.

I looked up at Braun, but there was no sign of his beast. Just calm, controlled Braun.

"He's... he's dead?" I had no doubt Braun had more experience with death than I ever had. "How do you know for sure?" Maybe I was in shock. Maybe I was a worse nursing student than I thought because I'd asked the crazy question.

He looked at me, and there was no fear in his gaze, no upset. Just acceptance. "My integrations enhance my vision. I can see no electrical impulses traveling within his heart."

"His heart stopped?" I looked down at Kevin again as the police officer stood, raised a radio he had attached to his shoulder to his lips and said a bunch of numbers which probably meant something to him and—

"Don't move. Either of you. Hands where I can see them."

Braun hadn't been moving to begin with, and he remained still now.

"He's not the bad guy. He is," I explained, pointing a shaking finger at Kevin. "He broke into my place while I was at class and was stealing my stuff."

The two officers might have heard what I said, but they'd never come across anyone of Braun's size before. They looked a little freaked. One was in his forties, gray hair and mustache. The woman was younger, maybe my age.

"You saw the truck in the parking lot with my couch in it," I added.

"Is that why you pushed him down the stairs?" the older officer asked.

I shook my head. Stunned. "What? No. That's not what happened."

"He's the guy from the show, the Atlan," the female officer said. "The alien."

"I don't much care what planet he's from. Homicide's on the way. Coroner, too." The older officer walked up the stairs slowly, hand on his firearm like he was ready to use it. "You two, on your knees. Hands behind your head," he ordered. "Now!"

Braun did as told.

"Wait!" I got in front of him. "He hasn't done anything wrong."

"Ma'am, you, too. On your knees."

"Me? It's my apartment."

"And there's a dead man on the stairs. On your knees. Now."

Even with my legs shaking, I knelt beside Braun, my hands up in front of me.

"Angela Kaur of Earth is innocent. There is no reason to be hostile toward the female," Braun warned.

"We don't know exactly what happened here." The older officer spoke.

The female officer was glaring at Braun. "And you're an alien."

"Yes, I'm aware I'm not from this planet."

"So?" I asked. "That doesn't make him dangerous. Kevin's the one hyped on drugs and breaking and entering."

"He's also dead."

"It's all right, Angela." Braun turned his stoic gaze on me. The way his jaw was clenched and the tendons in his neck taut, I knew he was pissed. And yet he was restrained as usual.

The older officer took a pair of handcuffs from his utility belt and cuffed me behind my back. Braun growled, but I caught his eye and shook my head. "Don't, Braun. They're just doing their job."

"You will not harm the female," Braun ordered despite the fact that the police were firmly in charge here.

As for Braun, the younger officer tried to put a pair of handcuffs on his wrists. "Shit, the cuffs are too small. What the hell do we do with an alien?"

"Hell if I know. Call the show. They'll have to have someone meet him at the station so they can figure out what to do."

"Do not call the *Bachelor Beast* program organizers. I am no longer associated with the show."

I whipped my head around to look at Braun. He wasn't with the show? Why? Was it because of me? What was going on? The police officers spoke over our heads as if we weren't even present.

"Alien or not, we'll have to take him in for questioning."

"I don't think he'll fit in the back of our squad car," the woman said.

"Shit," the other muttered, slowly shaking his head.

"I'll call the Interstellar Brides Program's testing center. They deal with aliens all the time."

I was panicked, the sight of Kevin's glassy eyes making me wince every time I glanced in his direction. He'd done this to himself, but I still felt badly for him. He wasn't a nice guy, but he didn't deserve to die. Not like this.

A tear dripped onto my cheek, and I used my shoulder to brush it away. Braun watched me.

"He is not worth your tears, Angela. He would have hurt you again and again," he murmured.

"I know."

Braun's gaze softened, and there was that look I was growing to depend on. Maybe even to love. "Your heart is too gentle."

"I can't help it."

He nodded. "You are a healer. I am a warrior. I will protect you if you allow me."

I nodded. Yes. I wanted that. I wanted him. Even with a dead man outside my apartment, handcuffs on my wrists, and two police officers looking at me like I was suspect, I felt safe. Thanks to an alien.

Life was weird and wonderful and full of surprises.

"Homicide is five minutes out."

"Good." The older officer looked down at us. "You two don't move. Got it?"

Neither of us said a word, but I leaned in close to Braun, and when he wrapped an arm around me, even the police didn't dare order him to stop.

11

THEY REQUESTED something called a paddy wagon to collect me. I had no idea what it meant, but it was a vehicle large enough to transport me from Angela's apartment to the police station. Angela had been taken away first by the original pair of law enforcement officers. Since one was a female, I'd been reassured for her safety, although my beast was not happy she'd been restrained *and* removed from my sight.

I'd growled in fury but forced my beast down. I would be of no help to her if my beast took over.

I had no idea the rules on Earth about situations like this. The human had tripped and fallen of his own accord. An accident. I would ensure Angela remained innocent of any wrongdoing. It was my fault he'd retreated from her apartment. I'd allowed my beast to come out and lost control, even just a little.

The human, Kevin, had hurt her in the past. Not physically but emotionally. He'd stolen from her. Stolen from her brave grandfather. And then when I returned to claim her, he'd been in the act of stealing from her again.

Angela was too small and kindhearted to be a threat to a human like that, but he'd been afraid of me. I didn't like bullies, and I would protect my mate at all costs.

It seemed that the cost was now quite high as she was being questioned and held separate from me.

They'd placed me in a cell, not sure what to do with me. I'd kept my beast controlled, as usual, and offered them no reason to feel threatened. Without handcuffs, there was no way for them to ensure I wouldn't do anything dangerous in an interrogation room. Thus, the cell. If they knew the bars were like sticks that I could snap with nothing more than a twist of my wrists, they would not have left me unsupervised.

There was nothing on Earth that could cage my beast. Nothing capable of stopping him.

Except Angela Kaur.

I had no clock, no way to know how much time had passed while I'd been in custody. There were no windows in this cold, sterile facility. It was a weak reminder of the prison cell on Atlan I would be in if I didn't get my cuffs on Angela's wrists soon. I could not do so from within these walls, and I could not do it without Angela's consent.

Thank the gods I still had her mating cuffs in my pocket, else my beast would be tearing this building apart to acquire them—and my mate.

Where the fuck was she?

No one had spoken to me. No one had questioned me. No one responded when I requested to see my mate. I knew nothing about what was happening outside the walls of this cell. My beast wanted to tear the bars down and find Angela, crouch over her like a clawed creature and kill anyone and everything that dared approach. But I was not a beast. I was an Atlan warlord, a male who had fought tooth and nail to keep my honor intact. I would not lose that battle now that I had found my mate.

I would not repeat my father's mistakes.

Pacing the small cell offered no outlet for my frustrations. I was at my limit when it came to controlling my beast. I'd never felt this out of control, this wild. I tugged at my hair, tried to move to bleed off the energy that was slowly growing in my chest like a storm's wind gathering speed. My beast was at the edge. I was at the brink.

How dare they keep my mate from me! Leave me with no answers as to her safety. Her welfare. I was a warlord with mating fever who needed to see his mate now. NOW!

Just as I was about to rip the bars from the walls, heavy footfalls came down the corridor, and Governor Maxim from The Colony appeared. With him was a female wearing the Interstellar Brides Program uniform. Ah, I recognized her from my initial arrival on Earth.

"I will not leave her," I muttered, guessing what might be to come.

"Easy," Maxim said, his hand up, as if that would stop my beast.

"Explain and explain quickly, Governor, or my beast will be set free to find my mate in this building."

He glanced at the female, then back my way.

"Shit, this is going to be bad." He sighed. I didn't like anything about his words, his tone, his stance. His presence.

The female, Warden Egara, spoke. "Warlord Braun, some say you have broken the laws of the state of Florida and of the United States. As you are not a citizen of Earth, you are outside the jurisdiction of their laws. Therefore the judge presiding over your case has determined that to solve this issue quickly you are to be banished from the planet and will be deported to The Colony immediately."

"Where is my mate? She will come with me," I replied through gritted teeth. I gripped the bars, ready to snap them if need be to get to her. I had no issue with leaving Earth behind. None. Their laws and the males who abused their females, those of Kevin's ilk, could go fuck themselves. The faster Angela and I were off this primitive planet, the better.

"Angela Kaur is still being questioned," the female said. "As acting warden in this area for the Interstellar Brides Program, I am the official liaison between the Coalition, the human police, and Governor Maxim. The humans do not want a spectacle involving an alien and neither does Prime Nial."

"Fuck. The prime knows about this?" Gods be damned, I was in more trouble than I had imagined. Prime Nial was the leader of the entire Coalition of Planets, the commander of the Coalition Fleet, and the final word on everything. His command was fucking law as far as the Fleet was concerned. And The Colony fell under his jurisdiction as we were all veterans who had fought in the Hive war. We weren't relieved of our duties and sent to our homeworlds. Technically I was still under Prime Nial's direct command.

"He does. And he does not wish for this incident to cause any problems with the Brides Program. If human females believe—even wrongly—that one of our males committed murder, the volunteer numbers will decrease and many warriors will suffer without their bride."

"Where is my mate?" I repeated. I had to leave. Quickly. I could not doom my fighting brothers to life without a mate because of the asshole human Kevin. "I will leave, but I will not leave my mate behind."

She kept her gaze on mine, not fearing the growl in my words. "She is not under arrest. She is being questioned as to the events of last night and will be released soon."

"Soon is not good enough. She is my mate," I said, stating the obvious. "No harm can come to her."

"No harm will come to your mate; however the events of last night have caused quite a mess. The person who was killed was not an unknown male. He was the son of a prominent state politician."

I gave a negligent shrug. "A grown man is not the responsibility of his parents."

She offered a nod. "That is true. In most cases. But the dead man's father, Colin Barrister, has a lot of both money and power. He is not happy."

"His son died in a tragic accident. I sympathize with his loss. It is a tragedy. But the man was illegally within Angela Kaur's quarters and stealing from her. From what she has shared, this is not the first time he has acted with such shame. If he had not been stealing her things, he would not be dead."

"That is all true. From what the police are gathering, he has... had a gambling problem."

"And other issues," I added. Now was not the time to lecture this stern-faced female on how a male of honor treated and cared for his mate, or any female for that matter.

"Yes. However, Colin Barrister has no intention of making his son's issues, or how he died, known to the world. They are going to bury the story, Braun, on the condition that you are not here to contradict them."

I narrowed my eyes. "What does that mean?"

"You are to be deported immediately," Maxim stated, breaking his silence at last. His tone said there would be no argument.

I turned my gaze to him. "I have done nothing."

"A human is dead. You were involved."

"As I said, Angela Kaur has done nothing except deal with a dishonorable man who stole from her."

She nodded. "Yes. I know. The police know. She will be free within a few hours."

I nodded. "Good. I shall wait for her."

"That cannot occur."

"What?" I gripped the bars, and they started to bend.

"Once the news is broken, there is to be a fourteen-day lockdown on all transport to and from Earth," Warden Egara said. "I will work with Coalition diplomats and local politicians, including Colin Barrister, to get this issue worked out to everyone's satisfaction."

"No." No. I didn't care what the warden said. I did not care what Governor Maxim said. And neither did my beast. Angela was mine. We would *not* leave her here.

"This is now an interplanetary diplomatic issue and all non-Earth citizens are being transported from the planet," Maxim added. "In order to maintain relations with the Coalition planets, you must leave here immediately. You will transport directly from this cell."

"No. Where is Angela?"

Before I could understand what Maxim was doing, he

moved toward the bars and slapped a transport beacon onto my chest.

I looked down at it, and my beast raged. Broke free. I wrenched the bars and tugged, needing to get to my mate, but the bars disappeared. They were gone and so was I.

From one second to the next, I was no longer on Earth but on a transport pad on The Colony.

"Mate. Now," I roared at Maxim.

He stepped back but didn't flee. He stood and faced me. "No. Calm your beast, Warlord."

"No." I was breathing hard, my fists clenched. I stormed down the steps and over to the controls.

"As Warden Egara said, all transport codes to Earth have been locked," Maxim said. "There is no way to get to the planet until Prime Nial and the human government come to an agreement.

I spun around, glared.

"You are banished from Earth. Listen, Braun. *Listen.*"

I tried to calm, but it was impossible. My mate wasn't just somewhere else in the building, but light-years away. Alone. With armed police officers surrounding her and no mate to protect her.

My beast roared, and I felt something I had not felt in years. I transformed, right there at the transport station. I kept the beast from smashing the control panel into pieces. Barely. That was our only way back to Angela.

"Mate!" I bellowed.

"Get Surnen down here," Maxim ordered. "Now."

The tech fled.

"The situation would be harmful to the entire Coalition if word of a human murder spread," he said, trying to appease me.

"Innocent."

He nodded. "I know. But that politician asshole is angry. Mourning. He wants to blame someone other than his own son. He has enough power to do this. It'll work out. Prime Nial has tasked his best ambassador with helping us. Lord Niklas Lorvar will do everything he can. He was recently mated to a human female as well. If anyone will understand your plight, it will be him. I've been told he is working closely with his Earth contacts to reopen transport channels. It won't be long, Braun. Just don't lose control. You know what will happen if you lose control. Angela will be lost to you forever."

Gods damned. Fuck. He was right, and the beast knew it. Even with the beast's acquiescence, I struggled to return to my normal form. After long minutes I could speak. "So, I am trapped here. And she is unprotected." I couldn't get to Earth. I couldn't get to my mate. The beast stirred, and had it not been for the cuffs around my wrists, I would not have been able to control him. Even with the cuffs, it was the beast who said her name. "Angela."

"She is fine. Safe. No repercussions will come from this upon her person. From what I understand, Kevin Barrister was found unresponsive in his bed. A seizure."

I didn't know what that was, but it was a lie. I didn't give a shit how the human government twisted the situation as long as Angela was safe.

"Mate."

"There is nothing to be done."

"Get her here." I pointed to the transport pad.

"She doesn't have your cuffs. There is no protocol."

I reached down and touched the cuffs hidden in my pocket, the solid strand still affixed to my belt. Had it only been a few hours ago that I'd gone to her apartment to claim her? And now I was on another fucking planet without her. Alone. She was alone.

"She is my mate. Change protocol."

"I have no power. No jurisdiction over this. I'm sorry, Warlord." He ran a hand over the back of his head. "I sent you there to find your mate, and now this has happened. I will do everything in my power to get you back to Earth to claim your mate, but until the transport ban has been lifted, I can do nothing."

I gripped the edge of the transport control station and yanked, ripping it from the floor. Sparks flew. My beast raged. Howled. So much for control.

We had other transport pads. They could fix this one.

And it was either kill the transport controls or take on a fully integrated Prillon warrior that I really didn't want to hurt. Maxim was more than my governor; he was my friend.

"Don't make me stun you, Warlord."

I whipped my head around at his words to glare at my leader, my hands holding the metal table. I was away from my mate with no ability to return to her. What would she think? Was she well? Safe?

He pulled his weapon from his thigh holster. I hadn't even noticed he'd had it on Earth.

"No mate. Shoot me." I couldn't get to my female, my mate, to protect her. The pain was agonizing, my fear for her mounting with every second, straining my control over my beast. "Do it, before I lose control."

"Damn you, Braun." Maxim was not amused.

That made two of us. I tossed the control panel across the room, and then, with one well-aimed shot by the governor of The Colony, the world went black.

12

I WAS EXHAUSTED. Overwhelmed. I could barely function let alone think straight. Kevin had broken in and tried to steal my things. He'd come from a rich, prominent family. He hadn't needed to steal the money I'd been saving for Gramps. Or so I'd thought. But I'd learned the more powerful and famous a parent, the more they were likely to lie to hide their flaws.

Colin Barrister was a prominent businessman and politician in the area. Kevin's father. He'd been charming and suave and wore designer suits and shoes that would probably cost me more than a month's salary to pay for. I'd only met Mr. Barrister once, and he'd been as perfectly fake as his spray tan. I was sure he had no idea what my name was, even after Kevin introduced us at a holiday party. He'd nodded, feigned interest for all of a few seconds, and moved on to speak to a senator or millionaire or something.

The vision had haunted me because that was when I'd seen the vulnerability on Kevin's face. The only time I'd seen that raw wound on display. Kevin had been nearly thirty and still trying to please the unpleasable parent. That look had bought Kevin an extra three weeks of pity dating, or at least that's how I preferred to think of it. He'd been sad and alone and lost. And I had a penchant for trying to heal broken things.

But not anymore. I was done with broken men. Broken aliens. Broken laws. I was tired of being surrounded by broken things.

I'd had no idea if Kevin's dad knew of his son's gambling debt, but obviously Kevin had been desperate enough to be stealing from me. Kevin had appeared to have more than enough money of his own, but he'd finally told me his income was tied to an allowance. Money his dad monitored.

That only made him more entitled than ever. Given anything he ever wanted, but supervised, had made him both lazy and paranoid that his disapproving father was going to take everything away. I was ashamed of myself for being sucked into his lavish lifestyle, which had been fake and empty, but I'd dumped his ass in the end. One more loser to add to the stack.

Until Braun, I'd not had the best of luck dating. But then, I hadn't chosen Braun; he'd chosen me. When I closed my eyes, I could still hear his deep, growly voice saying *mine*.

I couldn't wait to see him again. They'd told me at the station that Braun had been taken by a female named Warden Egara and another alien from The Colony. So I was waiting. My calls to the Interstellar Brides Processing Center had not been returned. No one would tell me a damn thing other than to confirm he had been transported. Kevin was dead because he'd stooped to stealing a fucking Crock-Pot and TV. I'd been pulled back into his sloppy life once again. Even though he was dead, he was still screwing with me and now Braun, too. Stupid Kevin had messed things up for both of us. But it had to work out. I just needed to be patient. Braun said I was his. He would come for me. Maybe the alien police had to question him, too? Maybe that's what was taking so long for him to come for me? Or maybe he had tried, and I wasn't home?

My apartment was a crime scene. I'd been handcuffed and taken to the police station. I'd been questioned for hours and released just before dawn. I had no idea what happened to Braun once the alien took him. He was not from Earth. He didn't understand our justice system or laws. He'd done nothing wrong except be there for me.

I'd asked the humans around me about him, but no one would tell me anything. Not the cops who'd brought me to the station. Not the detectives who'd interviewed me. Not even the public defender who'd sat with me and guided me through the questioning. No one had seen a huge-ass alien. There was nothing I could do except get a ride to the hotel and put on one of the uniforms that were reserved for new employees. I'd stock my cart and head to the VIP floor and start with Braun's room. Talk to him. Maybe he was there, sleeping. The idea of climbing into his big bed and curling up in his arms made me almost whimper.

I got to work, loading my cart.

"Did you hear?" Tina asked, passing me in one of the service hallways in the basement.

I rearranged a stack of folded towels on my cart so they

wouldn't fall. "What?" I glanced at her over my shoulder. Her eyes were wide and bright, and she seemed almost gleeful.

"There's a new bachelor beast!"

I stilled, swallowed. "What?"

She shrugged, but the smile didn't slip. "You heard me."

"Yeah, but... what?" No. That wasn't possible, was it? Where was Braun?

She looked left and right, and I forgot to breathe. "Roderick heard it from Jan, who heard it from Julio, who was delivering breakfast to the show's producers. That's all I know, but they're getting all the contestants together right now to give everyone an update."

At my apartment Braun had said he was no longer with the show, but that had been before we'd been arrested. Well, not arrested. *Questioned.* In handcuffs. If he wasn't going to be on the show anymore, could it be because of what had happened with Kevin? But if I'd been free to go, then so had Braun. He was innocent. He hadn't even touched Kevin. God, Kevin Barrister had to be the only guy unlucky enough to literally kill himself with a flat-screen TV.

I set my hand on her arm. "Where's the meeting?"

Her eyes widened behind her glasses. She was older, midfifties, with two small grandchildren and a husband who adored her. "What rooms are you cleaning today?"

I pulled out the piece of paper with my list, and she snagged it from me, skimmed it.

"In Beachcomber," she said, waving her hand. "Go. Find out what's going on, and I'll start on your rooms. But come right to me when you hear."

A burst of energy had me hugging her. "Thank you!" I called as I ran down the muggy hallway to take the stairs to the small conference room on the second floor. I was panicking inside. A new bachelor? That made no sense.

As I stood outside the closed doors, I took a deep breath, then another. My heart was pounding, and I couldn't just storm into a room. My job was to be invisible, and I had to act like it. I opened the door enough to squeeze through, then turned toward the corner where the water station was located. I pretended to organize the used glasses as I surreptitiously watched. And listened.

There were about fifty people in the smaller event room. The space was set up for a conference with rows of chairs facing a single table with three microphones and three chairs obviously set up for speakers. All twenty-four of the contestants were seated, although I didn't take time to count heads. Probably the show's staff filled in other spots. I recognized Chet Bosworth standing with a man and a woman facing them all.

"There will be a delay in production," the man said, and I assumed he was the producer. He glanced at Chet. "Longer than the one we already had. At least two weeks."

"But is there really a new beast?" one of the women called.

"Yes. He is an Atlan warlord, just like Braun. The governor from The Colony has not given me the name of his final selection yet, but he will be everything Braun was and more."

I snorted. No way. Sorry, mystery Atlan guy, but no. No one was better than Braun.

"The new warlord will arrive directly from The Colony *on the day we begin filming,*" the woman said and then cleared her throat. "He will not have time to do anything except change clothes and walk directly to the production studio."

"What? Why?" I heard multiple rumbles, murmurs of shock, and a lot of half-thought-out questions.

"Don't want to lose another one. That's two for two." One of the female voices said the words, and I realized they were true. Wulf to Olivia. And now Braun to me. All these gorgeous women and not one match yet. The show's producers had to be enraged.

The woman speaking held up her hands for silence, and the small group complied. "I have spoken to several of the warlords on a conference call, and I feel confident any of them would be an excellent replacement for the show."

"But what about Braun?" another asked.

Yeah, what about Braun? My heart caught in my throat as I waited for an answer. Braun should be sleeping right now, sprawled at an angle across the big bed in his suite.

"Warlord Braun has found his true mate and has returned to The Colony."

I froze. Tried to swallow. I outright stared at the producer now, not even pretending to do anything but listen.

"Found his mate?" It was Room 1214 who spoke. Unlike the others, she stood when she asked her question. She looked sleek and perfect. And bitchy.

Chet Bosworth cleared his throat, raised his hand as if to rub his eye, then dropped it quickly. "Yes."

"You mean he's been matched?" she asked, then glanced down at the other ladies around her. Whispers began.

"He's found his bride, so yes," the male producer said. "He took his mating cuffs and wears them now. He is off the market, ladies. But not to worry, we have another most eligible bachelor on the way."

Everyone started to talk at once.

Braun had found his mate.

Braun had found his mate.

Braun had been matched.

He had gone *back to The Colony*.

God, he hadn't gotten the first flight out of town. No. He'd transported *off* Earth. Gone meant really, really gone.

My heart thumped, hard and heavy. Then cracked. He'd left the planet? Been matched? But what about me? What about... everything we'd shared? The sex? Visiting with Howard?

"That's not fair," Room 1214 said. She may have even stomped her foot on the carpet, but I couldn't see the lower half of her body to be sure.

For once I was in complete agreement with her. It wasn't fair, but there wasn't a damn thing I could do about it. He'd found his mate. His *true* mate. That was what Chet had called her. His true, as in one-and-only, destined, love-of-his-life, fated mate.

I couldn't compete with that.

"How?" she asked. "I mean, he was in the hotel with all of us. When could he meet someone else?"

Chet sighed and lifted his hands in a hopeless gesture. "I am not an expert on aliens, ladies. Obviously the show hasn't had much luck with them, especially after what Warlord Wulf did to the set. If Braun has found his mate, then he must have been notified. I have to assume he'd been tested and matched through the Interstellar Brides Program. All I know is that I got a call this morning telling me he was gone, that he had returned to The Colony to be with his mate and that a replacement would be coming."

I had no idea if he was speaking the truth or not because

if there was anyone sleazy and cheap, it was Chet. But the producers weren't denying any of it. All they cared about was the show, the production schedule. If Braun was still here, they'd go with him, not wait until a new bachelor beast was identified. They were too lazy to do otherwise.

Talking started again, louder this time. I wasn't the only one stunned. I was, I hoped, the only one who'd been with Braun. Who'd taken him to meet her parents. Who'd slept with him. Who'd fucked him in my shower. And on my couch. And the floor. And the side of my bed. And in my bed. I was the only one who'd slept with his big arms wrapped around me, making me think everything was going to be good and happy and full of love.

And I'd believed the lie, even after we'd been arrested together. I'd believed in him.

The woman at the front cocked her head and shrugged. "Ladies, if Braun found his mate, then it never would have worked with you. Unlike guys here on Earth, Atlans know. Their beast knows. You should be pleased for him, but excited that a new warlord might be yours."

Talk kicked up again, but there was excitement now. Braun was old news. Out of sight, out of mind. If there was no shot at a match, they were done with him.

Did that mean I was done, too?

"We can't even say goodbye?" someone called.

Yeah, I wanted to at least say goodbye. Didn't I?

The trio in the front looked at each other. "He has already been transported back to The Colony. There is no mention of him ever returning to Earth."

Oh. My. God.

One of the glasses slipped from my fingers and dropped to the floor. It was muffled by the carpet, but a few heads turned my way. I picked it back up, then walked out of the room and to the service stairs. They were deserted, but I could hear the clanking of dishes below. I leaned against the cinder-block wall and took a deep breath. Tried to figure out what was going on.

Braun was on The Colony. Light-years away. He wasn't coming back. He'd found his mate. He'd been matched.

Was that what he'd meant the night before? When I'd let him into my apartment, he'd said he had something to tell me. I had noticed the large, beautiful cuffs around his wrists, but I'd hoped he'd been wearing them for me.

Back to the wall, I slid down until I sat on the top step and sobbed. I'd been so stupid. He had never fucked me with his beast. That's the one thing that had never made sense. All the times he'd touched me and held me and made me come all over his cock, he'd never let his beast out. Not like when Warlord Wulf had trashed a camera crew and taken his new mate up against a closed door on live television. Braun had never lost control like that. And now I knew why.

I wasn't his. The man might have enjoyed my body, but his beast had not been interested.

Now he was gone. Forever gone. Off-the-planet gone. He'd told the police officer he wasn't with the show anymore.

Had he come over to tell me he'd heard a match had been found? From the TV show's previews, I knew he'd been tested by the Interstellar Brides Program several years ago, but no match had been made.

Until now. Had he come over to offer me the courtesy of telling me that?

Of course he'd leave as soon as he could. He'd been to

my place to say goodbye, but the fuckup with Kevin had held him up. God, he'd almost gotten into big trouble that could have kept him from his mate. From going home.

I leaned my forehead on my knees. I wasn't his. I didn't belong to Braun. Some other female did. Were they together now? Had his match been transported from Earth to meet him on The Colony? Or was she from some other planet? An alien woman? A human? Was she tall? Was she beautiful? Were his cuffs already about her wrists? Was his beast soothed and happy with her? Was he fucking her and claiming her while I sat here and cried in a stairwell?

Of course he was. She was his perfect match. I knew all about the Brides Program, how nearly perfect the matches were. It wouldn't be any different for Braun.

Braun.

Tears burned down the back of my throat, forming too fast for all of them to escape from my eyes.

I'd known him for two days, and I was devastated. Heartbroken. Lost.

I'd thought—stupidly—that we'd had a connection. That what we'd shared had been special.

He hadn't even said goodbye.

———

Braun, The Brig, The Colony

"I am going back to Earth," I said, storming to the bars. I'd woken up in the cell, this one more than strong enough to keep my beast locked within.

"You can't." Governor Maxim stood just outside my cell,

his human mate, Rachel, and his second, Captain Ryston, flanking him. Rachel had her arms wrapped around one of his, and her head was leaning against him as if she were offering support of some kind.

"Let me out of here."

He shook his head. "Not until you listen. I'm sorry I stunned you, but you gave me no choice. It took four men to drag your ass down here." He waved a hand around. In all the time I'd been on The Colony, I'd never known the brig to be used.

Until now.

"I've done nothing wrong. I need to protect my mate." I looked at Rachel in the event she did not know my mate was a human female like her. Perhaps hoping she could talk some sense into her stubborn Prillon mate on my behalf. "My mate is Angela Kaur, and she's still on Earth."

"Braun, as I told you, the death of that human caused an interplanetary incident. Earth has locked out all transport until things are settled. *All transport* to Earth has been shut down because of this."

"The human was a wastrel who stole from my mate. He was verbally abusive."

Maxim's eyes narrowed, and his fists clenched. He didn't like a woman being harmed any more than I did. "He was also well connected."

"If Earth's justice system holds any worth of honor, that would not matter."

Rachel sighed and I turned to the small female. "That is true, Braun," she murmured. "Unfortunately it does matter. People with power and money can get away with just about anything. Not all the time, and there are good people fighting against them, but Earth is not perfect. Not by a long shot."

"Earth's issues are not mine. I have to get to my mate."

Maxim looked down at his feet, then back at me. "I know. I'm working on it with Warden Egara. We are going outside of the diplomatic circles. If we can make it happen, we will."

"If?" I was losing my mind. My beast raged, my fever pushing me to the brink. My beast pushed against me, and I began to grow.

"Shut that beast down."

"No," I countered.

Maxim glared.

I glared back.

"There is nothing I can do until they open up transport once more."

"How long will that be?"

"At least fourteen days."

"Are you serious?" Head bowed, I focused on the pain coming from my mating cuffs. That pain was Angela. A reminder that she was mine. She was real. She was out there, and she needed me. I would never reach her if I lost control. "Promise me she's safe. Swear it to me."

He nodded. "Prime Nial knew you would be upset. Even though everyone's been pulled from Earth, he has assigned an Everian Elite Hunter who has been stationed at the Brides testing center to watch over her until we can get her off the planet. She is being protected, and since he's not legally allowed to be on Earth, she—and everyone else on the planet—will never even know he is there."

My beast was not happy, but the news that an Elite

Hunter guarded her calmed him enough that I could think. And listen.

"How long?"

"I don't know. I am hoping Lord Lorvar is as silver-tongued as Prime Nial claims. I am going to do everything I can. I sent you there to find your mate. I will not deny you. But you must be patient."

I growled. "My beast is not patient."

He sighed. "I know. I will let you out of here, but I don't want to hear you've put a Prillon and two Viken in the med unit fighting in the pit to bleed off your rage."

"Mating fever."

"I don't care. You keep your shit together or you lose her. You hear me, Warlord?"

His words were true, and I gave a grunt in reply. I heard him. I didn't like it, but I heard.

"I am sending you on the next mission that requires an Atlan of your abilities. I'd rather you rip the heads off the Hive than my warriors in the fighting pit."

I grunted again. The idea of going into battle and destroying the Hive tamed my beast. Slightly. I thought of Angela on Earth. Alone. I hadn't had a chance to talk to her, to explain. To tell her she was my mate. That my cuffs were for her. If that loser hadn't been at her apartment, she'd be mine right now. She'd be here with me.

If the dishonorable male, Kevin, were not already dead, I would rip his head from his shoulders anew for keeping my mate separate.

I went to the bars and faced Maxim just as I had on Earth. "I will do as you say. I will continue to tame my beast until you gain me transport back to my mate. But you must do something for me."

He raised a dark brow, crossed his arms over his chest.

"Angela Kaur's grandfather," I said. "His name is Jassa Singh Kaur. He is a warrior. A warlord in his own right. He fought the enemy. Lost a leg but came out alive."

Maxim lifted his chin. He understood a fighter of honor.

"He is unwell. I do not think he will recover from his illness as Earth is primitive and Angela said his medicine is costly and most likely ineffective. He requires a ReGen wand."

"I can't get—"

"Warden Egara can," I said, cutting him off. "I'm sure there is one within the Brides testing center. I want it used upon him. Heal the veteran. It is my duty to ease Angela's suffering. He is a warrior of honor, and she loves him with her tender heart. If he dies, she will be heartbroken, and I cannot bear to think of her in pain. Not when something as simple as a ReGen wand can heal the elder."

Maxim studied me. "Done."

I nodded. "Get me on the next transport to Earth. In the meantime, send me on a mission. I must soothe the beast or I will be headed to the execution chamber on Atlan instead."

13

*a*ngela - *Two Weeks Later*

THE POLICE RELEASED my apartment two days after the incident. Two days after Braun left. There was no way I could've stayed with my parents that first night. They'd have asked too many questions, and I hadn't had any answers even though I knew more than most after listening in at the hotel. I'd just wanted to climb in bed and cry. And cry.

Since my BFF Casey had still been in Paris, I'd let myself into his apartment—we'd traded keys eons ago—and stayed for three days. I'd called in sick for work because there was no way I could clean the VIP floor and listen to the contestants gossip. While I'd wanted to skip school, I couldn't do it. I'd come this far and taken so long that I wasn't going to blow my degree now.

Just because an alien had swept me off my feet, given me more orgasms than I could keep track of and made me happy in just two short days, didn't mean I was going to turn into a Miss Havisham and live in an attic the rest of my life.

I'd showered and pulled myself together. Went to class.

Then I'd gone back to work. Back to my apartment, which I was going to move out of as soon as the lease was up. Everywhere I looked in the place, I thought about Kevin. More importantly, I thought about Braun.

I'd held off my parents for a week, but when they'd heard about the bachelor replacement on TV, I'd had to call and explain it all. Which had me crying again, but I'd pulled myself together and remembered Braun was happy now with his mate. He deserved happiness after what he'd survived. I remembered the integrations he'd shown us, the stories he'd told about his capture. How he'd escaped.

If anyone deserved a mate and children and a full life, it was Braun. What hurt was that it wasn't with me. I was selfish in my thinking since we'd only known each other two days. Two days and I'd expected him to be mine!

Now who was the stupid one? Me.

So I'd pushed through all my sad shit and got back to work, focused on school. Life.

Tina met me as I was stocking my cart for my shift. "I sure don't miss those contestants," she said, offering an exasperated sigh. "Sending them home until the new bachelor shows up was a smart move by the producers. God, who knew twenty-four women could be so whiny?"

She'd told me they'd moped about because Braun had found a mate, or they moped because none of them were her. Either way, they were a hot mess.

She shook her head, and I gave her a small smile. I was happy to avoid those women, although once the new bachelor did arrive from The Colony, it would be crazy at the hotel once again.

I gave her a small smile.

"What's the matter?" she asked, patting my shoulder.

I hadn't told her about me and Braun and had no plans to. It was my secret, the two days I'd think back on as... magical. Wild. Hot as hell. There weren't any cold winter nights in Miami for those thoughts to keep me warm, but I still wanted Braun to be mine. Just mine, even just for a little bit. I felt like whining too.

"Nothing, just not feeling great."

She humphed. "What floor do you have?"

I pulled out my slip with the list of rooms to clean. "Six."

A waiter pushed a tray past us toward the service elevator. I frowned. "God, those eggs smell awful."

Tina pushed her glasses down her nose and eyed me, then laughed. "Honey, if I didn't know any better, I'd say you're pregnant. My niece Carla went off all kinds of smells when she had little Michael." She shook her head and walked away, pushing her cart down the long hall toward the service elevator on the south side of the building.

I stilled, a pile of washcloths in my hand.

Pregnant? As if.

I set them on the lower shelf of the cart, then froze.

Holy shit.

Abandoning my cart, I went to the wall outside the HR department where there was a calendar, stood there, and stared at it. Twenty-six, twenty-seven... thirty-three, thirty-four.

"Oh my God," I whispered, putting my hand over my mouth.

I was late. I was *never* late. I was on the birth control pill! I couldn't be pregnant because that was the pill's job.

But I was. I knew I was. And I'd forgotten to take my pills for a couple of days. The days I was with Braun and the two days after when the police were breathing down my neck and Braun had ditched me for his one true match out in space.

I missed him so much my chest felt like a motorcycle was parked on top of me.

The nausea hit then, and I dashed for the bathroom down the hall, making it just in time. When I was done, I returned to HR, headed into the office, and told them I just threw up. They pushed me out the door, panicked I might spread some kind of stomach flu.

Yeah, what I had wasn't contagious. I had to know. I drove to the nearest drugstore, bought three pregnancy tests and a bottle of iced tea to chug on the way home.

Thirty minutes later I had my answer.

Sitting on the tile floor of my bathroom, I pulled out my cell and dialed Casey. "I'm pregnant."

Somehow.

"Holy shit," he whispered. "I'm in a meeting, otherwise I'd be there now. Meet me at my place at seven tonight and you can tell me everything."

"Okay," I said, my voice small, a tear sliding down my cheek.

"It's going to be all right. We'll figure this out."

His reassurance was weak, and I had no idea how anything was going to be all right.

I was pregnant. With an alien's baby.

Holy. Fucking. Shit. I was carrying an alien's baby. An

alien who was mated to someone else. An alien who didn't want me.

———

Braun - The Colony, Transport Room

I STOMPED down from the transport pad to stand directly before the governor.

"Well?"

He looked to the transport tech, who nodded, then back at me.

"I'm glad you were able to leave your group," he said, taking in my battle armor and the weapon I was only now tucking into my thigh holster.

"Your comm said I could get to Earth," I reminded him. "I pushed through a tier of Hive Soldiers and got to the Nexus Unit that controlled the entire group. His head is on the way to IC now."

Maxim crossed his arms over his chest and made a decisive grunt. "Perhaps if every fighter had such motivation, the war would be over."

I was breathing hard, not from battle but from the message I'd received. I was to return to The Colony immediately for transport to Earth.

It had taken sixteen days for him to get me back to Angela. It was about fucking time. My beast had pushed us through four different missions in that time, but I was barely remaining sane.

"I am to leave now?"

Glancing over Maxim's shoulder, there was Warlord

Bahre and five other Atlans. They nodded to me and went up to the platform.

"I've been working with Warden Egara, the human you met when you were jailed in Florida. Lord Lorvar, Prime Nial's ambassador, has personally settled the issue—"

"There's no issue. The guy killed himself."

"—enough so that Bahre or another warlord can proceed with the *Bachelor Beast* program. We have told the human authorities that the additional warlords are being sent to work as guards at the processing center."

"And?"

"And you will join them. You are not on the official transport list, but you Atlans are all so large that adding one more to the transport won't bring any notice."

"You're transporting seven warlords to Earth and you don't think anyone is going to notice?" I asked. This was a bit insane.

"One of them—and they are free to choose among those who are going—is to go directly to the *Bachelor Beast* television show and participate there. The others are to remain at the Brides testing center."

"I don't need five warlords to help me find Angela."

Maxim actually chuckled, a rare sight on a grumpy Prillon warrior's face. "They are doing something my mate calls a walkabout."

"Walking where?" I looked up at Warlord Tane, Bahre, and the other friends I'd made here. "There's not much walking to be had. Especially in Miami. The city is closed in and smells of swamp."

Tane grinned. "We're going to find mates."

Bahre chimed in. "Worked for you and Wulf. Fine females. Worthy mates. We tire of waiting."

I was the one chuckling now. "The humans will not be pleased to know rogue warlords are wandering around their planet looking for females."

Maxim crossed his arms. "That is why we did not ask permission."

My smile was genuine as I walked up onto the transport platform to join my friends. My first smile in sixteen days. "Good hunting."

"Thank you," Tane replied. The others grinned at me in silence as Maxim spoke.

"Warden Egara is waiting for you, Braun. Upon your arrival, she will take you to Angela Kaur immediately. You have four hours, Warlord. Four hours to get your cuffs on your mate and transport back with her. The window will then close once more and there will be nothing I can do. The bureaucrats are still arguing, and I do not know when we will be able to open transport again. At this time only Lord Lorvar is allowed to make transport arrangements."

"Four hours?"

He nodded.

I didn't need to be told more. Bahre slapped me on the back, and I looked to the tech. "Let's go."

"Warlord," Maxim called.

I glanced at him, and he tossed something at me. My mate's cuffs. I caught them easily. Fuck, I'd have gone to Earth and forgotten them. I didn't carry them into battle with me, so I was thankful Maxim had retrieved them from my quarters.

"Thank you," I said to my leader, then looked at the tech. "Transport now."

The tech looked my way, wide-eyed and scared, then

scrambled with the controls. I felt the vibrations and sizzle; then we were on Earth.

Thank fuck.

As Maxim had said, Warden Egara was waiting for me. She looked exactly as she had two weeks earlier. Same hairstyle, same uniform. I stalked over to her, ignoring Bahre and the others. They had their own personal agendas.

So did I.

"Warlord Braun. It is good to see you again. If you'll follow me, I'll take you to your mate."

She gave me a small smile, but she didn't linger. I had to assume she recognized the importance of my limited time here on Earth. She walked away and I followed.

Once outside, I breathed easier. The sky was dark, the barest sprinkle of stars visible and not even a fraction of what I knew existed out there. I had no idea what time it was, but I hoped the dark meant Angela would be asleep. I wished to find her in her bed. Naked, ready to be claimed. My beast was excited and eager to get to our mate. For the first time in sixteen days, he wasn't roaring to kill or maim. He wanted to fuck.

"I'm sorry about the size of my car."

The small vehicle beeped when she pushed a tiny button in her hand. I opened her door, then went around and climbed into the passenger seat, just as I'd done with my mate. I didn't give a shit that my knees were in my nose. I just hoped this small machine could move quickly.

"This is not a sanctioned mission. You are not officially here on Earth, so I couldn't make any accommodations for you."

"I am thankful for any help you offer."

We didn't say anything further, just drove through the

city. However, when she stopped the car, I did not see Angela's familiar quarters.

"First floor. This building. Number four on the door." I looked in the direction she pointed. "I will remain here in the car." She looked at the clock on the dashboard. "You have three hours and thirty-five minutes until the transport window closes. You *will* be gone by then."

She gave me a pointed look, and I had to wonder if she had children or had been a commander of some kind. There was no hesitation on her part in dealing with me, an Atlan warlord in mating fever.

"This is not Angela's home."

"No. It's not. I couldn't risk missing her, so I had a friend track her cell phone signal. She's here. Trust me."

I sat in silence for a few seconds, staring at the building where my mate waited for me, safe. Secure. I owed the Elite Hunter who had watched over her a debt I could never repay.

"Is the Hunter here?" I asked.

She shrugged. "I have no idea. You know how they are. Like ghosts when they want to be."

"Angela's grandfather?"

Now she did look at me, and her gaze was soft for the first time since I'd met her. She was quite beautiful, and I wondered why she did not have a mate to protect her.

"I took care of your request. Jassa swore not to tell a soul. He is healed." Her gaze drifted from me to the apartment. "Angela's heart will not be broken on my watch."

"Thank you."

She said nothing, so I nodded and exited the small car.

Time to make Angela mine.

14

ngela, Casey's Apartment

IT WAS dark outside and I knew it was too early for pajamas, but I didn't care. This was a freaking emergency.

"I would offer you some wine, honey, but you really shouldn't drink in your condition."

"I know." Grumpy and upset and fighting back tears—*again*—I reached for the small pint of my favorite ice cream and stuck a spoonful of the creamy treat into my mouth. Washing it down with warm tea was the best I was going to get. What I needed was about ten shots of tequila to send me into oblivion. Then I wouldn't have to think about Braun or his face. Or his kisses. Or the way he smelled.

Somehow his super swimming sperm were as powerful and stubborn as he was, because my birth control had been no match.

I was pregnant with an alien baby and had no freaking

idea what to do about it. I couldn't go to my doctor and tell
her I had an alien growing inside me. *That* wouldn't go over
well.

I couldn't go to my parents about this... well, I could. I
would, but not yet. I wasn't sixteen. I was a full-grown
woman and I was pretty sure they knew I had sex, but
having a baby made that fact real. But even if I *did* tell them,
what was I going to do?

How big were Atlan women? I had to assume so much
bigger than me. What size baby did they have? How the
hell was I going to fit an Atlan baby out of my vagina? On
Earth?

Again, what the hell was I going to do?

Casey settled on the couch next to me, and I scooted
closer, leaning my head on his shoulder. He had changed
out of his work wear—designer suit and tie—and put on
sweatpants and a T-shirt. Both our feet were bare. This
wasn't our first sleepover, and I knew it wouldn't be the last.
As best friends went, he was pretty freaking spectacular.
He'd even brought me the fancy Parisian shoes I'd
requested.

"I don't know what to do." I'd already told him about
meeting Braun, about our two days of nonstop sex, Kevin's
accident, the police. What I'd overheard about the show.
Braun leaving me behind like old news as soon as he'd been
officially matched to an Interstellar Bride. Everything. I'd
shared it all and cried my eyes out. Every freaking day since
Braun had left. Now I was crying because of not just Braun
but a *baby.*

Casey wrapped his arm around me, kissed my forehead,
and leaned his head down on top of mine. Gently he took
the ice cream from my hands and set it back on the table

next to my tea and his glass of dark red wine. "And you're one hundred percent sure?"

"I took three tests."

"Okay." He squeezed me closer, and I gladly accepted his warmth, the soft movement of his hand up and down my arm soothing in the best possible way.

Braun was gone. He wasn't coming back. But at least I wouldn't be alone. Right? I'd thought about ending the pregnancy, but giving up the one piece of Braun I had left... I just couldn't do it.

I loved him. How that was possible after such a short time, I had no idea. But I was in love, and pregnant and alone with no hope of changing either situation. It wasn't like I could get on a plane, go to Braun's house, bang on his door, and tell him everything.

He was gone. Like outer space gone.

"I can't believe this is happening to me."

"I can't believe that fool left you," he muttered. "He's obviously an idiot not worth having."

I didn't know why, but I felt I had to defend Braun. He'd done nothing wrong. Hadn't led me on, made any promises like a Regency duke. "He found his mate. He's an alien. It's different with them. I'm happy for him. In the saddest way possible."

"If I weren't gay, I'd have married you the day we turned eighteen."

His obvious lie made me laugh. "We would have been divorced in a month."

"Oh, but what a marvelous month it would have been."

The familiar banter made me smile and actually did help. Casey had been with me since my first day at a new school in the fifth grade. I'd been the new girl with a weird accent, and he'd been bullied for being who he was. Even then, the other boys knew he was not like them, and they made sure we both knew we didn't belong. We'd teamed up, stood up for one another, and been best friends ever since. I trusted Casey with my life. No joke. The fact that he was also a genius businessman and world traveler didn't hurt either.

"What am I going to do?" I asked.

He took a deep breath, and I knew before he opened his mouth that I was not going to like what he had to say. "First, you are going to stop crying. You are going to be a mother and that little peanut—"

"Little peanut? There's no way an Atlan baby's ever been compared to a little peanut."

"—is lucky to have you as a mother."

"True." I already adored the baby, and I had no idea if it was a boy, a girl, or an alien beast with fur. I didn't know, but I wrapped my arm around my abdomen with a fierce need to protect my child. But when I thought of me and Casey in school, how we'd been picked on—and we'd been human— I didn't want this half-Atlan child to go through any of that. Of course, if he, or she, turned out to be Atlan big, it wasn't like there'd be any issues on the playground.

Still...

"Then you are going to waltz into that Interstellar Brides Processing Center and you are going to demand to speak to someone in charge."

"Why?"

"Because, love, this baby does have a father. And he has a right to know."

"Oh God." I'd only been thinking about myself. How was I going to deal with this? What was I going to do? How much I missed Braun. I'd been so busy imagining him with someone else that I hadn't thought about telling him. "You're right." Braun was gone, but he was a good man... alien... male. Whatever. He was good and honorable and gentle. He would be an amazing father. But... "What if they make me give up the baby?"

Casey's arm squeezed me again. "Well, if the child is an alien who can turn into a beast, would the little one really be able to live here, on Earth?"

"No. No. That's not fair. But I'm not sending my child into outer space."

"You could go out there. Maybe find another mate? Another Atlan to help you raise the baby?"

I wanted Braun. But he wasn't an option. Maybe I could find another guy. Another gorgeous Atlan who made me hot and made me laugh.

"I could ask." But I didn't want to. I wanted Braun.

The tears burst from me like I hadn't cried in years. Casey held me. And when I lifted my face to look up into his eyes, I didn't even try to hide my pain. "I don't want to do that. I want *him*."

"I know. I'm so sorry, love." He leaned down and pressed his forehead to mine for a brief moment before placing a lingering kiss there as well.

He was right. What if my baby was a boy? A little Atlan beast? What if he changed into a beast in school? Hurt someone? I had no idea what might happen. I didn't know how big the baby would be, how long I would be pregnant. Nothing. I knew nothing.

I had to go to the processing center and send word to Braun somehow. I needed medical information. Advice. A checkup. I needed to know what to expect, what had happened to other human women who had Atlan babies. Surely I wasn't the only one.

But none of that was going to happen tonight. I lay my head on Casey's shoulder and reached for the remote.

"What do you want to watch?" he asked.

"Anything but romance." I grinned through my tears and grabbed the ice cream. "Sci-fi? Let's watch some badass marines kill some aliens."

Casey chuckled and I felt almost normal. Almost.

———

Braun, Outside Casey's Apartment

I covered the distance to door number four in record time. These dwellings were in better repair than the building Angela lived in. I assumed that meant the humans who lived here had more wealth. Number four was on the ground floor, and I was grateful not to have to face the bleak gray stairwell just a few steps away. I hadn't been given any updates as to the repercussions of the thieving human's death, although I had to assume Angela had been cleared of all responsibility. I should have asked, but my beast had been impatient to leave for Earth.

Since the warden had brought me here instead of a jail cell containing my female, I assumed all was well. If Angela had been incarcerated, I would have snapped the bars and taken my mate from the building. Once she was on The Colony, Earth laws would not be an issue.

The light was on in the apartment, the golden beam coming through the large window that was to the left of the entry door. I paused on the threshold when I saw her. Fuck, she was more beautiful than ever. Her dark hair was pulled back from her face, and she was in a simple shirt and shorts as she sat upon a large sofa. She was looking at something in her hands, lifted a spoon loaded with a dark and creamy food to her mouth.

I'd never before wished to be a spoon.

I took one more step toward her, hand raised to pound on the door, then froze.

She wasn't alone. A golden-haired man came from the kitchen, smiling. He carried two drinks and said something I couldn't hear through the glass. Coming up behind her, he kissed the top of her head. She turned and smiled up at him. I saw trust in her gaze. Affection.

He kissed the top of her head.

After, he dropped down on the couch beside her and set the beverage he'd been carrying for her on the table before them. She looked unhappy, no joy or pleasure on her face as she turned to him for comfort. She leaned forward and set whatever she was eating next to her beverage.

Then the male leaned in close, wrapped his arm around her shoulder, and she settled against him like she belonged there as he stroked her arm. As she allowed him to hold her.

Just as she had with me.

The male nuzzled her hair with his lips and placed another kiss there. And another on her forehead. Their faces touched, and he was looking deeply into her eyes, their discussion obviously intimate and very personal. Familiar.

Fuck.

By the gods, she'd chosen another.

My beast broke. For the first time in years I felt no rage, no fire burning in my veins.

Nothing. I was a stone statue. Cold. Empty. Without hope.

The man huddled close and looked down at her lap and she cried. Something was hurting our female, and she turned to this male for comfort and protection.

Him. Not me.

My beast roared to break down her entry door and rip the man's head off, just as I'd done with the Hive a short time ago.

She was mine.

Mine!

Yet I had been gone for over two weeks. I hadn't said goodbye. Hadn't made my intentions known. Clearly she had found another. I continued to watch as they huddled together and chose a vid to view on the human's television.

Angela wasn't upset I'd left her. She had laughed. She was smiling. Cuddling.

With. Another. Man.

I turned away, unable to look at the scene inside the apartment a second longer. I could knock, tell her she was mine, but I would not tear her from her happiness, even if it wasn't with me.

This man made her smile. He kissed her freely. He was human and here. To be with me she would be forced to leave the planet. Leave her parents and the grandfather she loved with every ounce of her heart. This human could give her that.

I was just a beast who killed Hive. Whose beast was done being held back. I was finished penning him in. For years—*years*—I'd kept the beast under control. No longer.

I would not let Angela see me like this. My beast did not rage; he broke open.

No, she'd made her choice, and it wasn't me.

I strode down the steps and back to the warden's vehicle. Tucked myself into the seat beside her.

"What's wrong?"

"She's found another."

I looked blindly out the front window.

"Another? Another Atlan? Impossible."

"No. A man. A human male with golden hair. He was kissing her."

She whispered under her breath. "You're sure?"

I looked to the woman who'd been so helpful. "Yes. Quite."

She sat and stared at me, but I could tell she was thinking hard.

I was numb. My beast was taking over more and more by the second. I had to remain in enough control so I could fit within her vehicle. If I grew to my beast size, I would have to punch out the roof.

"You can go in and talk to her. Ask her. Make sure. There has to be some mistake," she said.

"No."

"Tell her how you feel."

"No."

"Warlord," she all but begged with that one word.

"She has moved on and so must I," I replied. "This human can make her happy. She can remain here, on Earth, with her family. I cannot offer her such comforts."

She sat quietly for another moment. "You wish me to take you back to transport?"

"Yes."

She turned the vehicle on, then pulled out of the lot, returning the way we'd come. I'd had hope on the journey here, but now that hope was gone.

"I'll have you back to The Colony soon," she murmured, her voice soft.

"No. I wish to be transported directly to Atlan. To the prison. It is over. It is time I faced the truth. I will follow the same path as my father."

"You don't have to *die!*" she exclaimed, stopping at a traffic light.

"I am an Atlan. I have mating fever. I have no other options." I held up my cuffs, the ones that should be around Angela Kaur's wrists. "I lost my mate. I've made my choice. My beast has chosen as well. There is no other possibility for me now but execution."

15

ngela, Interstellar Brides Processing Center, Miami

THE WALLS WERE thick like concrete slabs that absorbed sound. The air smelled strange, a mix of batteries and cleaning supplies mixed with chalk. Maybe it was my pregnancy nose that picked up on the odd combination. The receptionist in the lobby had been nice enough. Still, I had no idea what to expect as I waited in the small meeting room, but it was not the unfriendly female who entered.

She looked human. But then, did that mean she actually was? I had no idea. Other than what I'd seen on the *Bachelor Beast* television show, I had no idea what was going on out in space, who was there or what kinds of aliens existed. Not once had I considered volunteering to be a bride. So, like most humans, I'd pretty much ignored everything to do with aliens and war and brides. I had enough problems at home.

Like a sick grandfather and parents who depended on me. Nursing school. Work.

And now... a baby. An alien baby.

"Ms. Kaur. I am Warden Egara. I am in charge of bride processing here in Miami. Why are you here?" She was beautiful, probably in her late twenties with dark brown hair and startling gray eyes. Her gaze was direct. Intelligent. The look of someone used to being in charge and making difficult choices. But the way she had her arms crossed over her chest made it clear she wasn't eager to see me. Maybe she'd had a rough day, I had no idea, but I got not-happy-to-see-me vibes.

Her gaze narrowed when I hesitated. "I don't have a lot of time. What do you want from me?"

Yeah, not happy to see me. I blinked, taken aback by her open hostility. "I'm sorry?"

"Why. Are. You. Here? Do you wish to volunteer to be processed as an Interstellar Bride?"

I frowned. "No."

She sniffed and rested her hands on the back of a chair, but did not bother sitting down. I wondered if it was because she never sat, didn't want to wrinkle the dark gray uniform skirt she wore, or because she simply didn't like me. Which made no sense. I had never met the woman.

Gray eyes focused on me like lasers, and I started shaking. Again. Tears were coming, too. I could feel them, but I swallowed hard and forced them back down. "I... I need your help. I need to get a message to an Atlan. Warlord Braun? Do you know him? Know where he is?"

"Indeed." She crossed her arms again, still scowling. "What kind of message?"

My hand dropped to my abdomen as if I instinctively

knew I needed to protect my baby from this mean woman. This was who they had greeting nervous new brides? This was the last face one would see before being whisked away into outer space?

No wonder they had so many advertisements on television and the Internet. No wonder they were seeking volunteers by showing off a hot alien first. Warden Egara was a scowling, mean, unhappy bitch. Yet she was my only chance to reach Braun, to let him know about our baby.

"I need to talk to him. I know—" I held up my hands to interrupt her when she opened her mouth to speak, and rushed the words out of my mouth before I lost my courage. Again. I had driven here three times in the last two days. Pulled up. Parked. Turned my car back on and gone home. I had never been such a coward in my entire life. But this was scary. An alien baby. Alien lover who didn't want me. Not knowing if I'd be able to stay on Earth. Not knowing *anything*.

"Please. Let me get this out."

Warden Egara looked down her nose at me from where she stood, but my knees were too weak to risk standing. I was shaking like a leaf.

"I know Warlord Braun found his one true mate and left Earth. I know. He came to my apartment with his mating cuffs on and said he needed to tell me something but didn't get the chance. He's gone. He found a mate. I heard them talking about it on the show. I don't expect him to want me back, because he's happy on The Colony or Atlan or wherever. I'm happy for him with this female. I might not look it, but I am. He deserves it. But that's not why I'm here."

The warden opened her mouth again, but I spread my palm wide in front of her face and rushed the rest of the words out. "I know. He's gone. It's fine. I'll deal with it. But... but I'm pregnant. The baby is his. I know he has a real match now and he went to meet her and claim her. I don't expect him to be mine. But he's a good man—Atlan—whatever. Braun is good. He has a right to know he's going to be a father."

I stumbled over all of that and took a deep breath. There, I'd done it. Shared the whopping secret that would probably end with me locked up in Area 51.

"What?" Her voice had lost some of its edge, but what did she mean, *what*? Was I stuttering?

"You do speak English, right?"

Her brows came together. "Of course."

I spoke slowly, just in case she was a bit dense today. "I. Am. Pregnant. With Braun's baby. Okay? I took three tests to be sure. I know he has a mate now. I know he was matched. But he needs to be aware of the baby. And I need to know what to expect. This baby is half human and half Atlan. Will they let me raise my child here? On Earth? How long will I be pregnant? Is it forty weeks gestation, like a human baby? And will I be able to deliver the baby? How big will it be? I'm almost done with nursing school, but none of my textbooks or clinicals cover this. If we stay on Earth, will the baby turn into a beast? Will Braun have visitation rights? How will this work? And what if his new mate doesn't accept this? I don't want to expose my baby to someone who won't love him." There. I'd said it again, even more in depth. She had to understand now. That about did it, right? "Or her. It could be a girl. I don't know yet."

"What?" she asked again. All anger slipped from her face, and she just looked shocked. Yeah, a human having an alien baby was a surprise.

She sank into the chair next to mine on one side of the small meeting table and took my hand in hers. Her entire demeanor changed from wicked witch to caring friend. I blinked with confusion but didn't pull my hand from hers when she spoke again. "Angela, I think we got off on the wrong foot. For that, I'm sorry. Start from the beginning and tell me everything."

I didn't tell her *everything*, but I told her enough. She knew *how* I got pregnant, I was sure. When I was done, she was leaning back in her chair, arms crossed, the angry glint back in her eyes. "You've left out something important."

I stared at her, confused. "I did?" What? I had no idea.

"What about the man you were with three nights ago? The blond? First floor. Number four."

What the hell was she talking about? "You mean Casey?"

"Is that his name? Your lover? The man you ran to with your troubles. The man who was holding you? Kissing you when Braun came to find you?"

I stared. And stared. Processed. Freaked. "Braun came back for me?" My heart leaped, and my pulse pounded. "Why? Why did he come back?"

"There was finally an open transport window. He came back to claim you, Angela. And found you with another man. You betrayed him."

"Casey is not a man!" I shot out of the chair. This time it was me looking down my nose at *her*. "I mean, he's a man, but not *my* man. How dare you? Casey is my best friend. He's been my best friend since the fifth grade. And he's not my lover. He's gay!"

She pursed her lips. "Then why did he kiss you?"

I was going to punch her in her perfect little nose. That's what I was going to do. "He kissed me on the forehead! We watched sci-fi movies and ate ice cream while I cried my eyes out because my alien lover has found a mate and I'd never see him again. Oh, and I was carrying his baby! Let me tell you, I needed that fricking ice cream. I love Braun. I did not betray him! I love him. Why?" I all but moaned. "Why would he think that? Why didn't he stay and talk to me? Ask me?"

Her face leached of color. "Oh, dear."

"He was here? And he didn't talk to me? Didn't even ask?" I shoved the chair out of my way and took a step closer to her. "You were there, too. Weren't you?"

"I drove him to your place."

"And you didn't talk sense into him? Or look into that fucking window yourself?"

She stood and began pacing. "I'm sorry, Angela. Atlans, especially those in mating fever, do not always see reason."

"But he has a mate. He left to meet her."

She shook her head. "He met his mate, yes. *You.* He went to your apartment to claim you, but there was the incident with your ex. He was deported from the planet."

"They said he found a mate! That he was matched."

"He was. *You are his mate,*" she said again.

Oh. My. God. "Call him. Comm him! Whatever you aliens say. Right now. Tell him the truth."

She shook her head. "I can't."

"Why not?" Whatever. I didn't care how, I just needed to talk to him. Now. "Then send me to The Colony. I'll talk to him myself."

"I'm so sorry. When he saw you with the other man— well, he didn't go back to The Colony."

A sick feeling twisted in my gut as the dramatic advertisements for the *Bachelor Beast* program appeared in my mind. The show had made a very big deal about the fact that an Atlan warlord who failed to find his mate was executed. Find love or be put to death. It was so dramatic. So fantastical.

It couldn't be true. "No."

"Yes."

I was going to vomit and not from morning sickness. Faint. Scream. "No. It's not true."

"He transported directly to an Atlan prison for execution."

"Is... is he dead? Did they kill him?" I whispered, barely able to get the words out.

"I don't know." She wrung her hands, clearly upset. "The Atlans don't *want* to kill their bravest warlords. It's not their intention. They want happy mates. Families. My understanding is that they will keep him for a few days at least. Parade females before him one after another, hoping his beast will take an interest in one of them. A last-ditch effort."

So, Braun might be dead. Or he could be choosing another mate right now? And all because I'd had a sleepover with my best friend, let him kiss me on the forehead, and that big idiot Atlan had assumed I chose Casey as my mate?

No. No. No. I grabbed the pretty little warden by the front of her shirt and pulled her close enough to snarl in her face. She was a good bit taller than I was, but fury gave me strength.

"Braun is mine. I want him. I love him. I'm having his fucking baby," I practically snarled. Maybe there was a little bit of beast in me, too.

He hadn't chosen another. He'd wanted me, too. That's

what he'd come to tell me when Kevin had been there. But he might already be dead.

"Find out where he is. Now. And send me to him. I don't care if the king of all aliens doesn't want me to go. I'm going. Got it?"

"Got it." She was smiling like a giddy fool. This woman made no sense at all. Maybe she really was an alien. "Let's find your mate, Angela. But I must warn you, he will not be Braun as you know him. He'll be in his beast form. You'll have to deal with his beast."

"I'm not afraid of Braun. I don't care what form he's in."

"Excellent." She walked to the door and opened it. "Follow me. First, you'll need an NPU so you can talk to everyone in space. After that, we'll talk to transport. While you are not wearing cuffs and technically not mated to an alien, you are carrying an alien baby, which gives you a first-class ticket to outer space. The transport pad should be available this time of day."

I followed her and swallowed down my terror. I was going to transport to another planet and face down a hurting, angry beast.

16

ngela, Planet Atlan, Prison Block 384

I WALKED between Tiffani and Warlord Deek, their presence on either side of me the only thing keeping me from losing my nerve as we passed cell after cell of screaming, raging, roaring giants. Beasts.

I'd transported to Atlan, and this couple, one human and one Atlan, had met me and escorted me to the prison. Warden Egara had sent Tiffani to her mate, and they had stayed in touch. Now here I was, walking past raging maniac after roaring monster. Intimidated didn't begin to cover what I was feeling.

Was this what was waiting for me? A snarling, destructive giant? Would I find Braun with fists bloodied from pounding the walls of his cell? Skin scratched and bruised from throwing himself against the invisible barrier that somehow held these gigantic, furious creatures inside their cells?

Tiffani reached for my hand, and I held on, squeezing back with twice the pressure she'd applied to me. I was probably crushing her poor bones. She didn't complain. "It's going to be okay, Angela. I was just like you, although I'd been matched. Deek was locked in one of these cells, and I had never met him. But his beast recognized me. He knew I was his mate."

"You. Mine." Deek had transformed into his own beast minutes after we stepped into the prison block, and snarled threateningly at just about every cell we passed. Apparently he was feeling very protective over his mate. Tiffani had grinned at him, patted him on the cheek, and told him he was handsome and sweet and adorable.

"And you are mine, lover boy."

A beast slammed into the cell's energy barrier on Deek's left. I jumped. Tiffani ignored the roar. Deek turned and roared back twice as loudly. If Tiffani thought that was sweet and adorable, she must truly be blinded by love.

I thought he looked scary as hell, but Deek wasn't my beast. Braun was. Or at least, I hoped he wanted to be. I'd been so relieved to find out he wasn't dead yet that I hadn't really thought too much about what was going to happen once I got here. To Atlan.

To him. And his beast.

What was I going to do if he was in a rage? I knew he would never hurt me, or at least I believed it up until that raging monster had tried to smash his body through the prison cell wall.

Tiffani watched me. "You're going to be fine. Trust me. It's going to be all right. Braun will recognize you."

I gave a shaky nod. "I know he will. But then what?"

She eyed me. "You've had sex with him, haven't you?"

"Yes." I thought the question was a bit personal, but this was not exactly a normal situation, and Tiffani was the only human woman I had access to who had actually been mated to a beast. "But not with his beast."

"What?" Tiffani stopped walking. Since our hands were still joined, she pulled me to a standstill as well. "You had sex with him? He told you that you were his mate but he never showed you his beast?" The alarm in her voice made me start to shake.

"No."

Tiffani looked up at Deek. "Why? Why would he do that?"

Deek shrugged. "Scare mate. Control." His gaze focused on me, and I had to look up—way, way up—to ask my questions.

"So Braun didn't show me his beast because he didn't want to scare me?"

His huge shoulder went up and down in the beast form of a shrug. "Run away. Small female. Too small." His gaze slid to his own mate, Tiffani, who not only was significantly taller than me, but her body was twice the size of mine, overflowing with lush curves. Tiffani noticed her beast's lingering inspection, and her cheeks turned a cute shade of pink.

"Deek. Behave."

His jaw clenched. "Mine."

She giggled, then looked at me with a mix of mischief and anticipation in her eyes. She was practically glowing with happiness. "We better hurry. I know that look."

I glanced at Deek and realized I knew that look, too. The

way his beast was eyeing Tiffani was the same way Braun had looked at me right before he thrust his cock deep and made me beg for more. "Oh boy. Okay. Let's go."

They escorted me to the cell where Deek had been told we would find Braun. The interior was shadowed, as if Braun didn't want to bother with the light. Still, the corridors were well lit, and I could see him.

I had expected to find a raging monster like what we'd passed in the other cells. A bloody, roaring creature so out of control the Atlan's only option was to put him to death.

"Let me in there." I spoke to Deek, but I couldn't look away from Braun's bare back, from the shine of the silver integrations evenly spaced up and down his spine. He faced away from the corridor, curled onto his side like a wild animal who had been hurt and was dying. He didn't move. Didn't even turn his head to see who passed by outside of his cell. It was like he was already dead.

Deek walked to the control panel on the side of Braun's cell and stood still. When he took too long, I tore my gaze from Braun to look up at him. "Let me in there. Now. Hurry up!"

Deek tilted his head and stared, which was somehow much more serious coming from a beast than it would have been had he still been in his more normal form. Even then, he was big. Like Braun. Big and muscled and handsome. Now, he was so serious and focused. "Must be sure."

I nodded, but apparently that wasn't enough.

"Female. Mate. No help. You go in. No help." The jilted way of speech struck me as odd, and I wondered if the NPU device Warden Egara had given me was working properly because I didn't understand what he was saying. I looked to Tiffani, who was nervously biting her lower lip.

"He's right, Angela. You need to know. If you go in there and he gets violent, no one will be able to help you. It will be too dangerous. A beast with a female to protect is even more dangerous than those we just passed. If Braun loses his shit, you're going to be on your own."

I blanched, becoming a little worried. I'd come all this way to help him, I sure as shit wasn't going to back down now.

"You went into a cage just like this, didn't you?"

"Yes."

"And you and Deek had never met? Right? You'd been matched, but he didn't even know who you were?"

She nodded. "I'd been tested and matched to a guy already here, ready for execution. I was insane. I know. But—"

I cut her off. "I know Braun. He's mine. He's not going to hurt me." I held Tiffani's gaze until she nodded. She turned to her mate.

"Let her in, Deek. Then take me home."

His growl of agreement would have made me laugh if I weren't so nervous. I talked a good game, but I was worried. Why hadn't Braun ever shown me his beast? If he truly thought I was his mate, then why hadn't he claimed me right away like Wulf had done with Olivia—on live television? The sounds of sex coming through that closed door had been so hot I'd practically cheered when the live broadcast kept right on going.

But that was Wulf. And Deek was Deek. Braun? I'd never met his beast.

The energy barrier opened up next to where Deek stood, and I walked into the cell. Tiffani gave me a little wave right before Deek put the barrier back in place.

"Good luck. We'll come back and check on you later."

I nodded and pivoted on my heel to face my future. Or lack thereof.

Braun stiffened on the large pad where he'd been lying, as if finally sensing me. It looked like a soft mattress, and I wondered if they didn't get beds because the beasts would destroy them or use the materials as weapons.

Not that they needed a club or long stick to kill someone. Not when they were eight feet tall and solid muscle.

I bit my lip. "Braun?" I took a step forward and stopped, unsure what to do. I had thought long and hard, and I wasn't going to tell him about the baby. Not yet. He had to want me for me. Just me.

Braun lifted his hands to his ears and covered them as if he was in pain. His roar made my heart leap into my throat and I startled.

"Braun? It's me. Angela. I transported here from Earth."

He roared again, but I was ready for it this time.

"Braun?"

"No!" His voice was deeper, so low that I felt the vibration in my chest.

What the hell was his problem? "What do you mean, no? I'm here. Aren't you even going to talk to me?"

He swung his legs around, lowered his hands from where they covered his ears, and stood slowly.

I watched, my neck craning as I looked up and up and up.

He was even bigger than Deek. More than eight feet tall. "Holy shit." The words popped out of my mouth before I could sensor them. I'd expected big, but good God. "Braun?"

He turned to face me, and I held perfectly, completely still as he approached. He wore only pants. No shirt, no shoes, as if those things were no longer needed here. When I was squarely before him, he leaned down and inhaled deeply, his nostrils flaring. His gaze raked over my body as if to confirm I was really here, as if the voice he'd been hearing hadn't just been in his head. That done, he lifted his huge hands and wrapped them around my back, then pulled me flush to his body. "Real. Mate. Real."

I wrapped my arms around his waist—well, as far as I could reach—and held him. "I'm real."

He lifted me then, off my feet and into his arms so we were face-to-face. "Gold man. No. Mate. Mine."

Gold man... gold man. Ah, Casey and his blond hair. My heart ached for Braun now, for the confusion. The mistake. For what he thought he saw and the fact that he'd almost died believing something false.

I placed my palms on the sides of his cheeks, leaned in until my forehead touched his. "The gold man, Casey, is just a friend. You are the only man I want, Braun."

"Mate."

I nodded, our foreheads bumping. "Yes."

He growled and walked to a section of the wall I hadn't noticed before. Halfway up was a cushioned shelf, and Braun settled my backside on it. It wasn't quite wide enough to sit on without being propped up, but it was close. Once I was there, he lifted my arms over my head. I glanced up as the cold shock of metal snapped into place around my wrists.

They were cuffs. His mating cuffs. And now they locked around my wrists with a finality that should have terrified me. Instead I felt relief.

He was mine now. Mine. The matching cuffs around his

own wrists confirmed our connection. There would be no execution. No losing him.

"Braun?"

"Mine." When I was locked into place, I realized what this perch was for. Mating. Claiming. Fucking. I was more than tied to the wall. I had metal cuffs locked around my wrists, those cuffs attached to metal chains that were anchored in the wall. There would be no escape, no changing my mind. No second chances.

Good. I didn't want to be anywhere else.

Braun waited, his gaze locked onto my face when I lowered my eyes from the cuffs to look at him. He shook head to toe, every muscle and ligament and blood vessel so taut as if ready to explode. His chest and shoulders were pulsing with the fight for control of his own body. He reached down, tugged open the front of his pants, his cock appearing like a club, thick and long. God. It was huge. And hard. Bigger than when we'd been together in Florida. Pre-cum already dripped from the tip as he studied me.

I was fully clothed. How was he going to—

Rip.

There went my pants and undies. He yanked the tattered fabric over my ankles and threw my clothes behind him like garbage.

Another rip and my breasts were bare and on display.

While he'd been rough with my clothes, he was being gentle with me.

"Mine." Hands on the insides of my thighs, Braun bent forward and put his mouth on me.

I jerked, gasped, and then moaned his name.

He fucked me with his tongue. No foreplay. No suckling. Just raw need. Lust. Hunger.

I was wet and aching in seconds.

Holding my legs wide, he suckled and tasted me, and all I could do was hold on to the chains for dear life and give in. Give him everything. "Braun!"

"Mate." His movements gentled for a few seconds, but his tenderness didn't last. He thrust two fingers inside my wet core and latched his lips over my clit with such force I screamed as the first orgasm struck like a whip on bare flesh. I had no resistance. I was not ready for the intensity of the pleasure.

He stood up, gripped the base of his cock, and thrust deep before I had a chance to recover. I cried out again because he was so big. If he hadn't prepared me, he would have been hard to take. He stretched me wide, filled me deep.

If I heard the other Atlans' beasts raging in their cells, then anyone in the prison could hear me being fucked. I was shocked to discover I didn't care who knew what we were doing. This little padded seat he'd put me on and the restraints indicated that this was the hope for all Atlan prisoners, that a mate would be found and they'd be saved. Sex was the only way out, and everyone knew that I was here to save Braun.

I. Did. Not. Care. I was free.

Chained to the wall with a beast fucking me, filling me, thrusting into me like I was the only female in existence. He wanted me. Only me.

Needed me.

I was all that would save him.

For the time apart, I'd been wrong, so wrong. He hadn't wanted someone else.

It had been me all along.

He proved it by his absolute obsession, his devotion to me—and only me. It was intense, broadcast with every grunt, every touch, every hungry thrust of his cock.

He didn't want me just because I was pregnant or because he liked the way I cooked or wanted to steal my rent money. He was mine in a way no one ever had been before. And I was his. I was saving him, and he was saving me right back.

His cock filled me until I thought I might sob if I didn't come again. "More. I need more," I moaned, my head thrashing against the wall.

He thrust faster, and I was grateful for the half seat that helped me stay in place.

"Mine. My pussy. Mate."

"Yes." I could fall in love with his voice alone. So simple. So deep. So hot. I rambled as another orgasm rolled through me, and I yanked against the chains. I needed him. Needed to touch him. I was dying. Dying from too much. Too much cock. Too much skin. His scent. The emotions exploding inside me. Dying.

"I love you, Braun. I love you," I breathed as he pushed me over the edge.

———

BRAUN

ANGELA. Mate. Mine.

The words played on repeat over and over in my mind, the beast's complete focus on our mate. Her scent. Her hot, wet pussy. The way she was splayed before me like a feast.

The mating cuffs on her wrists had ended weeks of my agony. I'd been prepared to die, to leave her to her happiness. Her life with the golden-haired man.

But she was here now. With me.

"Mine."

The beast was in complete agreement. I'd heard her claim that the male was only a friend, but the beast was not satisfied until the cuffs were on her wrists. Until we'd fucked her. Until she'd soothed my fever and made me whole because she was now mine.

"I love you, Braun. I love you..."

Her scent, her cries of pleasure, her pussy fluttering and clamping down on my cock as she found her release.

I was lost. My beast roared as I filled her with seed, claimed her in traditional Atlan custom for all time.

Anchored by her at last, the rage I'd carried in my blood for years, the fear that I would lose control like my father had, faded for the first time since I was a child, and the peace that settled over me was almost painful.

It was a silent, calm agony of relief.

Holding my mate, I released her hands from the anchors in the wall and gently inspected the mating cuffs to make sure they had properly adjusted to her wrists.

She looked from them and up at me. "They're perfect, Braun. They're beautiful."

Her words pleased my beast, and I leaned forward, content to hold her in place, cock buried deep, and curl my large frame around her. I held her for a long time, unwilling to move as her small hands stroked my beast. Me. My head, running her fingers through my hair. My back. Until finally she wrapped her hands around my face and gently shoved at me until I was where she wanted me, far enough away so she could look me in the eye.

Then she kissed my beast. She kissed us. Me. Him. The pain that had been flowing through me became piercing and leaked from my eyes in burning liquid.

"Oh no. Braun. Baby, don't cry." Angela kissed away my tears, and I held her. Kissed her as my cock hardened again inside her.

I took her lips once. Twice. Then thrust my cock deep once more.

"Mine."

She laughed, then moaned, and the movement made her body clamp down on my cock. I groaned. Thrust. Hungered. Needed. Loved. Adored. Worshipped. She was mine; this amazing, beautiful female was mine.

I fucked her once more until she screamed her satisfaction. Until her pussy pulsed and fluttered and she begged me to do it again and again. When she was tired, I held her in my arms, the beast sleeping with his back to the wall. He refused to recede, refused to allow me to cage him again after so many years of fighting to break free.

He held our mate. He tasted her. Fucked her. And he was content.

We were both content at last.

EPILOGUE

Angela, The Colony

I DIDN'T KNOW how to tell him I was pregnant. I'd only thrown up that one time in the hotel basement, and besides sore breasts, I didn't have any other signs that Braun might notice. After the claiming—God, that had been hot and wild —he was going to be upset that I hadn't told him. I could already hear him worrying that he'd been too rough with me.

For the first time ever, he hadn't held back. I'd seen the real Braun, the complete Atlan he was. His beast was fierce, but I'd known he'd never hurt me. An Atlan claiming, pressed against a wall, arms pinned overhead and taken hard?

My pussy clenched remembering how his dominance had made me come. But his beast hadn't been scary or overwhelming. Perhaps it was because my cuffs were around my wrists that he'd been soothed a bit. Perhaps it was because he didn't have to fight any longer. The beast was getting what it wanted, what it had been searching for all along.

Me.

I couldn't help but smile.

Braun gripped my hips and rolled us so I straddled him. "Is that a smile of satisfaction, mate?" he asked, looking up at me.

We were in his quarters on The Colony. In his bed. He hadn't let me far from it in two days.

His thumbs stroked over my bare skin, and I smiled down at him. The glint of his cuffs caught the light. "How could it be anything else?" I asked, running my hands over his broad torso. His skin was warm, the muscles beneath rock-hard. He was... perfection.

He smiled too, his eyes gentle. The difference between how controlled he'd been on Earth and now was so obvious. He'd held himself back, held the beast in check. No longer.

The beast and the Atlan were satisfied. Happy.

And yet I still hadn't told him of the baby. I could just blurt out the words, but I figured there would be the perfect time. The perfect way. What would he do when he found out he'd left me behind... pregnant? Would his beast rage?

I was enjoying this version of Braun. While he was careful with me, the claiming hadn't been the only time he'd been dominant and bossy. My pussy still quivered with the satisfaction he'd just given me. His cock was still buried deep inside me. I clenched down on his hard length, which had never softened.

Braun's pale eyes heated, and his grip tightened. "Mate," he warned.

As if I wanted him to deny either of us the pleasure that would come from him taking me. Again.

He lifted me up, lowered me onto him once more. I was so slick that my body offered no resistance. I leaned forward, slapped my hand on the wall above the headboard. My breasts dangled over his face. He lifted up to suck a nipple into his mouth as he began to fuck me. Again.

My breasts were swollen, my nipples ridiculously sensitive. The suction from his mouth alone had me close to coming. "Yes!" I cried, the sound bouncing off the walls of his room.

My pussy clenched and milked his cock, and he came with me. It was over within minutes, our need for each other satisfied again. For now.

I slumped down onto his sweaty chest, closed my eyes as I listened to his steady heartbeat. I'd never been this wild about sex. Not until Braun. Then again, he was so attuned to my body. Knew what I needed even when I didn't. Like during the claiming. Sure, his beast had been in control, but it had been a hard, wild fucking that I'd needed just as much as he had. The sounds I'd made... God. My cheeks got hot now thinking about how wantonly I'd behaved.

As soon as it had been over, the guards had seen the cuffs about my wrists as proof that his fever was gone, and we'd transported directly to The Colony. I'd blushed furiously on the way out of the prison and to the transport center. I hadn't been able to look any of the guards in the eye. I'd known going in I'd have to have sex with Braun to save him. No hardship there. I'd wanted him so badly it was as if I'd had a beast inside myself, too.

But after? Yeah, total mortification. While I figured the guards were honorable enough not to watch—the prison had to have cameras—they'd heard. I hadn't been quiet. In fact, I'd screamed my pleasure. Not once but twice. Up against a wall. Pinned. Fucked hard. Taken.

Braun, on the other hand, had grinned. Beamed. It hadn't been because the fever was finally over, although I was sure he'd been thrilled about that. It was because he'd satisfied his mate and everyone had heard her screams of pleasure.

God. Such a Neanderthal.

A beep came from the comms unit on the wall. Braun sighed. "Answer," he called.

"Warlord Braun, you and your mate are requested in the transport room at once."

Braun didn't even flinch or attempt to cover me as I lay naked and sprawled over him, so I had to assume the sound was for a pseudo-phone call, not a video one. He might be a Neanderthal, but us in a porno was something else.

"We're not leaving The Colony," he replied to the voice.

"No, Warlord. You have incoming."

Braun stroked my hair back, and I lifted my chin to look at him.

"Incoming?"

"Yes. Your mate's family is scheduled to arrive in... seven minutes."

I bolted upright, and Braun groaned when he popped out of me. "Oh my God. My parents are coming here?"

"Comm out," Braun said, watching me as I stood at the side of the bed and freaked.

"Seven minutes?" I looked down at myself. "Braun, I look like—"

"You look beautiful, mate."

"I look well fucked."

Braun grinned. God, he was so handsome when he did that. His smiles were coming more and more frequently, and it was, I knew, all because of me. I would ensure for the rest of my life that he did so often.

"You do."

I rolled my eyes at him and set my hands on my hips. "I don't want my parents to know what we've been doing."

He sat up, and God, those abs tightened and rippled. "We share mating cuffs. You traveled to a far-off planet to be with me. I think they may have an idea."

I pursed my lips, then spun in a circle. "Braun, where are my clothes?"

I had no idea what happened to the Earth outfit I'd been wearing when Warden Egara transported me to Atlan. I'd been wearing them when we'd arrived on The Colony, although a little ripped from Braun's aggression during the claiming, but that had been two days ago and I hadn't gotten dressed since.

"They are gone. You do not need such garments here."

"I'm not going to meet my parents naked!"

"I will make clothing for you, mate. Do not worry. I will care for you in all ways."

I frowned. "You're going to *sew* me some clothes in... in five minutes?"

"No. I will create them with the S-Gen machine." Braun slowly climbed from the bed. Smiling, he went over to the wall. Naked. He looked over his shoulder at me, raked his gaze down my body, then pushed some buttons on the wall. "Come, mate. The S-Gen machine must scan your body to make the proper size."

I rose eagerly, excited to see something outer space-y. Other than transporting across the galaxy, which had been awesome but I didn't actually get to see with my own eyes, this was the first gadget I'd been close to since my arrival. Braun had kept me... busy.

In the corner was a smooth black area marked with glowing green lines laid out in a grid pattern.

"Stand on the machine. The green lights will scan you for size."

"Okay." I did as he instructed. The green lights moved over my body like lasers. When it was done, I stepped down and held Braun's hand as we waited. Before my eyes a full set of clothing appeared, as if it had been transported directly from a seamstress to my bedroom.

"This is an Atlan female's gown. I wish to see you in it, if that is acceptable."

He was shy which I found adorable. I lifted the gown and smiled at the dark red color. I was going to look fabulous in this dress. "I love it."

I had no idea what else to say. A transporter that instantly made clothes. I realized as I put the soft garments on that they fit just right, too. The machine was magical.

"You need clothes too." He was just staring at me. "Hurry!"

He blinked, then grinned, then turned back to the machine and made an outfit for himself. It was only when we were both fully dressed—I'd been stunned stupid by watching Braun put on clothing—that I realized something, but it was too late now.

"Next time I want underwear," I told him.

He took my hand and tugged me out the door that had silently slid open. "Not a chance."

We walked down the beige hallway and turned a corner, the color of the stripe changing to a pale shade of blue. There were many corridors, and I doubted I'd be able to find my way back without Braun's help. Of course, I was distracted because my parents were coming.

Here.

The Colony.

Space.

On Earth, I hadn't even had time to say goodbye, so tears clogged my throat with appreciation.

Another door slid open, and we were in a familiar place. The transport room.

A tech stood behind the control table. A man with dark hair and a bloodred collar about his neck greeted us.

"Warlord. My lady. I am glad to see you both looking so well." He wasn't poking fun or being silly. He was serious.

Braun set his hand on my shoulder and responded with equal sincerity. "I apologize, Governor. You have not been formally introduced to my mate. This is Angela Kaur of Earth. Angela, this is Maxim Rone. I have him to thank for sending me to Earth."

The governor bowed to me. The governor of The Colony *bowed* to me. Was this a weird dream? I recognized the sharp lines of his face, the golden and brown skin and hair tones of his species made for excellent pictures, which was why they'd started putting up advertisements back on Earth. The gossip was, when you were matched to a Prillon, you got two of those bad boys.

No thank you. One huge alien was more than enough for me to handle.

The governor looked directly at me. "Thank you for your help in saving Braun."

"He's my mate." That was all I had to say on the matter. Apparently it was enough.

"My mate is Rachel, also from Earth. There are several other women, all brides from Earth, who are eager to meet you. I am sure you will be inundated soon enough, but they knew you'd be... occupied for a time."

I flushed. I'd been *well* occupied.

"Your family will be arriving soon. There has been a slight delay in the transport window."

"The diplomatic issues have been resolved?" Braun asked. His hand slid from my shoulder to around my waist, pulling me in close. I tucked into the crook of his arm.

Maxim nodded. "Yes. The ambassador dealt with any lingering issues."

The door to the transport room slid open, and another man entered. Man, alien... whatever. I recognized his race as Prillon. Like the governor, he also wore a collar about his neck. Unlike the governor's dark red collar, this Prillon's was a silvery gray. He was formal and stiff and bowed to me.

"I am Dr. Surnen. The governor spoke of your arrival, and I heard you would be in the transport room awaiting family. I wanted to take the opportunity to check on you personally."

"She is well, Doctor," Braun assured him. "I've seen to her personally."

I slapped Braun on the chest. "Hey!" I felt my cheeks heat. These guys could talk about sex as if it wasn't embarrassing.

"Yes, but in her—"

"Thank you, Doctor," I said, cutting him off. I widened my eyes and tried to silently tell him to zip his lip because I didn't want Braun to find out I was pregnant from someone else. I had no doubt the governor knew of the situation since he'd had to coordinate with Warden Egara. Obviously he'd told the doctor. And hopefully no one else. "I know that you wanted to ensure I wasn't weary from transport..."

The doctor remained still and studied me. He looked to Braun, who was almost placid looking. Then he nodded. "I see. Yes. I can tell that you are indeed well. If you have any issues or concerns with that—"

"Angela is strong," Braun advised, cutting him off. "She does not need observation because of transport."

Maxim looked down at the ground and covered his mouth with his hand. Yeah, he knew. Dr. Surnen knew. Braun didn't.

"No, you're right. She doesn't need me for that."

"I'm glad you're here though," Braun began. "Angela is a nurse on Earth."

Surnen's dark brow winged up. "Indeed?"

"Student. I did not complete my program," I clarified. "I was in my last round of clinical training when I met Braun."

"We are always in need of those with medical expertise. I hope that you will stop by the med unit soon. We have Coalition training protocols. You can begin immediately. I would be grateful for the assistance." He arched a brow again, gave me a pointed look. One, I was thrilled with the offer. I could be a nurse here, on The Colony. How cool would that be? I'd learn all about alien life forms, how to heal the warriors who came here, how to take out their integrations.

And the Earth women they'd just told me about? Surely they would be happy to have the option of a woman for their more... delicate... issues and concerns.

But none of that was what Dr. Surnen meant. I could practically read the alien's mind.

I want to check and ensure you and your baby are healthy.

I felt the vibration of the transport pad beneath my feet, felt the electricity in the air as the hairs on my neck went up.

"Transport imminent," the tech said, and we all turned to face the raised platform.

I blinked and there were my parents, Gramps, and Oscar.

The cat jumped from Gramps's arms and ran beneath the control table.

"What the hell was that?" Maxim asked.

"A cat," Braun explained, releasing his hold on me.

I dashed up the steps and hugged my mother first, then my father. When I got to Gramps, he squeezed me hard; then I pulled back and stared.

"Holy shit."

He grinned at me. Gone was the sickly pallor. His eyes were bright, his back straight. He was smiling and he looked... well.

"I know. I'm feeling pretty darn good!"

"What... how... you... that latest medicine has really helped!" I said, then hugged him again, but carefully, as usual. While I'd talked to my parents and Gramps after Braun left Earth, I hadn't seen them in the two weeks. I'd been too busy and too sad to deal with them in person.

"Ah, no need to be gentle. The cancer's gone."

I pulled back and looked to my parents. They were smiling and nodding, tears sliding down my mother's cheeks. "Outer space looks good on you." My mom smiled through her tears.

"What? How?"

"Your mate fixed me right up," Gramps said. "Got a lady in a fancy uniform waving a fandangle wand over me. Had a blue light and all. She did it a few times as we sat out back and fed Howard more beef jerky. I started to feel better right away. Which is why I can't stay long. Howard will miss me."

"Dad!" Mom said, although her usual frustration of his relationship with Howard was gone.

I spun on my heel, looked to Braun. "You did what? What wand?"

He walked over to the base of the stairs. I was just a tiny bit taller than he was where I stood, three steps above him. "I'd been deported. The transport window was closed. I didn't know if I'd get back to you. If I'd be executed. I couldn't leave a fellow veteran to remain ill just because he lived on a primitive planet." He looked to Gramps. "He served with honor and deserved to be healed." Braun met my gaze. "I couldn't bear to think of you in pain, mate."

Gramps tapped his prosthetic leg. "Does this make me a cyborg, then? I've got metal, just like you boys do."

Mom laughed harder and wiped her eyes.

"You did that for him?" I whispered.

"I did it for him, yes," Braun confirmed. "But I did it for you."

I couldn't be any more in love with my big, brawny alien than I was in this moment. I launched myself at him, and he caught me. Kissed me.

Everyone was laughing, and when we lifted our heads, we laughed, too.

I pulled back, looked into his face. "I love you, my brawny Braun."

He smiled then, rubbed my nose with his. "I love you, too. You were made for me."

"You have a busy day, Angela Kaur of Earth," Maxim said, breaking into our *moment*. "Your family will need to return to Earth in no more than three days' time, but the ambassador has arranged a permanent transport pass for your family anytime they wish to visit. Which I believe will be very often, especially in the near future."

I looked over my shoulder at the governor. "Thank you." Then I looked to my parents while Braun still held me. "I'm sorry I didn't say goodbye."

"You had good reason," Mom said, taking Dad's hand. "Being in love is... out of this world."

I rolled my eyes at her joke, and Braun put me down, although he seemed somewhat reluctant to do so.

"What does Maxim mean, mate? With your grandfather well, there should be no urgent need for visitation."

Maxim cleared his throat, and I looked to him, then to Dr. Surnen. Shit. This wasn't how I wanted to do this, but then again, I had no idea how I pictured telling my alien lover, my alien mate, that he was going to be a father.

I bit my lip, set my hand on my flat belly. My mother gasped, and I knew she'd caught on.

"Mate?" Braun looked worried. Confused. I couldn't bear to keep him in suspense.

"I... I'm pregnant."

Braun stared at me, his eyes widening. He remained still, and I wasn't even sure he was breathing. "What?" he whispered.

"I'm having your baby. I know it was a surprise and sudden but... well, I guess it was meant to be." I wasn't going to talk about his super swimmers in front of my family.

"Baby?"

I nodded. "Baby."

"You?"

I nodded again, starting to get worried. "Me. And you. Us. Are you... happy?"

"Happy?"

All of a sudden, his eyes rolled up into his head, and like a redwood in the flipping forest, he tipped over. Fainted dead away. The thump of him hitting the ground was loud, and from some hidden corner of the room, Oscar hissed.

Gramps laughed and came down the steps to wrap an arm around me as we stared down at Braun, out cold. Dr. Surnen knelt beside him and waved a wand over his face.

"The guy fought the Hive, survived being captured and integrated," Maxim said. "Escaped. Made it through Earth's stupid reality shows. Even lived through his mating fever. But fainted dead away because you're having a baby."

Gramps tipped up my chin and smiled.

"Not many people can fell a beast."

"My beast," I said, then knelt and took Braun's hand, tried to revive my stunned Atlan. As if deciding this was the best moment for a grand entry, Oscar walked to Braun and sauntered up onto the Atlan's chest as if Braun was his personal mountain. He curled into a ball and immediately started to purr.

I stared at my boys and couldn't stop smiling. "If this is what happens when he finds out we're having a baby, I can only imagine what he'll do if we have twins."

Gramps burst out laughing and caught Dr. Surnen's eye. "They do run in the family, Doc. They do indeed."

"I shall need to examine you immediately," the doctor replied, not in the least amused.

I shook my head. "Later." I leaned down and kissed my unconscious hero. He'd saved me in so many ways. I was ready to start my new life on a new planet with him and a new baby. Braun was my life now. Time to start living it. With him.

He just had to wake up first.

A SPECIAL THANK YOU TO MY READERS...

Want more? I've got *hidden* bonus content on my web site *exclusively* for those on my mailing list.

If you are already on my email list, you don't need to do a thing! Simply scroll to the bottom of my newsletter emails and click on the *super-secret* link.

Not a member? What are you waiting for? In addition to ALL of my bonus content (great new stuff will be added regularly) you will be the first to hear about my newest release the second it hits the stores—AND you will get a free book as a special welcome gift.

Sign up now! http://freescifiromance.com

FIND YOUR INTERSTELLAR MATCH!

YOUR mate is out there. Take the test today and discover your perfect match. Are you ready for a sexy alien mate (or two)?

VOLUNTEER NOW!

interstellarbridesprogram.com

DO YOU LOVE AUDIOBOOKS?

Grace Goodwin's books are now available as
audiobooks...everywhere.

LET'S TALK!

Interested in joining my **Sci-Fi Squad**? Meet new like-minded sci-fi romance fanatics and chat with Grace! Get excerpts, cover reveals and sneak peeks before anyone else. Be part of a private Facebook group that shares pictures and fun news! Join here:

https://www.facebook.com/groups/scifisquad/

Want to talk about Grace Goodwin books with others? Join the **SPOILER ROOM** and spoil away! Your GG BFFs are waiting! (And so is Grace) Join here:

https://www.facebook.com/groups/ggspoilerroom/

GET A FREE BOOK!

JOIN MY MAILING LIST TO BE THE FIRST TO KNOW OF NEW RELEASES, FREE BOOKS, SPECIAL PRICES AND OTHER AUTHOR GIVEAWAYS.

http://freescifiromance.com

ALSO BY GRACE GOODWIN

Rebel Mate

Surprise Mates

Interstellar Brides® Program: The Colony

Surrender to the Cyborgs

Mated to the Cyborgs

Cyborg Seduction

Her Cyborg Beast

Cyborg Fever

Rogue Cyborg

Cyborg's Secret Baby

Her Cyborg Warriors

The Colony Boxed Set 1

Interstellar Brides® Program: The Virgins

The Alien's Mate

His Virgin Mate

Claiming His Virgin

His Virgin Bride

His Virgin Princess

The Virgins - Complete Boxed Set

Interstellar Brides® Program: Ascension Saga

Ascension Saga, book 1

Ascension Saga, book 2

Ascension Saga, book 3

Trinity: Ascension Saga - Volume 1

Ascension Saga, book 4

Other Books

ABOUT GRACE

Grace Goodwin is a USA Today and international best-selling author of Sci-Fi and Paranormal romance with more than one million books sold. Grace's titles are available worldwide in multiple languages in ebook, print and audio formats. Two best friends, one left-brained, the other right-brained, make up the award winning writing duo that is Grace Goodwin. They are both mothers, escape room enthusiasts, avid readers and intrepid defenders of their preferred beverages. (There may or may not be an ongoing tea vs. coffee war occurring during their daily communications.) Grace loves to hear from readers! All of Grace's books can be read as sexy, stand-alone adventures. But be careful, she likes her heroes hot and her love scenes hotter. You have been warned...

www.gracegoodwin.com
gracegoodwinauthor@gmail.com

Printed in Great Britain
by Amazon